The Mission: North Korea

(A Military and Zombie Apocalypse Series)

3 Years After... Book 2

G.R. Mountjoy

Electronic Edition

Visit me at

http://www.wordpress.com/grmountjoy

and find me on FACEBOOK under G.R.

Mountjoy

Editing by:

Monique Happy Editorial Services
mohappy@att.net

Cover Art:

Steven Pajak

Dear Readers,

This is a work of fiction. All of the characters, organizations, and events portrayed in this novel are either products of the author's imagination or are used fictitiously. Any resemblance to real persons (living or dead), places or events is purely coincidental.

* * *

First and foremost, I would like to thank a whole lot of people. The first is my wife

Jennifer. You are my best friend, and I love you more every day. Thank you for everything. To my daughter Sarah Kate, your smile brings a tear to Daddy's eye every time I see you, and to the baby in Mommy's stomach, well I am sure you will be awesome also. To my friends who are not any part of, nor bear any similarity to any character in this book: You guys have shaped me into the person that I am. Thank you for always being part of my life. For all the good and bad, it has been a great ride. Who knew that we would all be friends 20 years after high school! To my family, thank you for the great upbringing and life that you provided for me.

As far as Book 1, there were great reviews, and there were some bad reviews. I learned to take them all in stride. I can tell you this much. There are some people out there that can be very kind in their words, and there are others that are not very kind. Thank you once again to those that were very honest, and to those that had the heart to be brutally honest. To Mark Tufo, thank you for telling me to get it out there, I was scared to publish it, but I did it, and thank you. To my editor Monique Happy, thank you for the diligent work and for working with my story, and also for tolerating my horrible grammar. To Mike McShea, the first cover was great, there it is in print, and you did an awesome job. To Steven Pajak, thank you for the second cover and the continuous work to make it what it became. If I forgot anyone I am sorry.

Thank you to the men and woman of our Armed Forces. If you think that I missed something, or didn't set it out exactly right, feel free to write to me. I can do this thing and write this story because of your sacrifice to this nation. I know that we sleep under the blanket of protection that you provide. I thank you for this. May God bless you and your families.

Thank you to Tim Brown "who is in no shape, way, or form related to or has any similarity to Big Brown in this book. Your friendship, mentoring, diligence as a co-worker, soldier, and recruiter are and always will be second to none.

Thank you once again to my wife, your friendship and hard work as a mother make me thank my lucky stars everyday.

To the readers, thank you for your purchase! I know that I am not the most grammatically correct writer, and to be honest I am not that great of a writer. I just hope that you enjoy what I have written, and feel free to contact me if you think that I messed something up!

To the Zombie writers out there that have inspired me and my story. Thank you for your hard work and great stories. Mark Tufo, Steven Pajek, Z.A. Recht, J.L. Bourne, Jessica Meigs, Shawn Chesser, John O'Brien, Joseph Talluto, Stephen Knight, Peter Clines, Bryan James, Todd Sprague, Craig Dilouie, Bonnie Dee, E. E. Knight, Christopher Golden, and every writer from the Star Wars Universe. Your work has given me many hours of great and interesting reading.

G.R. Mountjoy

Dramatis Personae

Colonel Ryder "Achilles" Mountjoy USA, Delta Force, Seeker Element Commander

Major Kris "Meat" McGilvra, United States Secret Service, SEAL Team 6 Retired

Chief Warrant Officer 5 Scott "Hollywood" Riloh, USMC Force Recon, Army Aviator

CSM (R) Mathew B. "Moon" McShea, US Army Special Forces, NSA EOD

Chief Warrant Officer 3 Eric "Opie" Lyons, US Army Special Forces, ICE Agent, 18D Special Forces Medic

Sergeant First Class (R) Tim "Big Brown" Brown, 101st Airborne Division, Army Sniper

Sergeant Joshua "Little Brown" Brown, 101st Airborne Soldier, Sniper

1st Lieutenant Ryne "B" BeMiller, Delta Force, 18A Special Forces

First Sergeant Dave "Mac" Long, Delta Force, Special Forces Weapons Sergeant

Doctor Christopher "Stewy" Baker, Seeker Element Virologist

General David "Honcho" Smith, Chairman of the Joint Chiefs of Staff, Secretary of Defense, Unites States of America

President James "Eagle" Striker, POTUS

Doctor Dickie Lyons, Nurse Practitioner USS Chung Hoon. Civilian Doctor

Captain Josiah G "Tripp" Teeple, Skipper of the USS Chung Hoon

Baron Snydor, Civilian Mechanic

Agent Chris "Smoke" Rahe, CIA Operative South Korea Branch

Agent Ryan "Ghost" Snyder, CIA Operative South Korea Branch

The Mission, North Korea

Chapter 1

The Boat

As the Osprey V-22 Boeing Aircraft
made its way out to open water to the
rendezvous with the USS Chung Hoon, the
team was busy relaxing and looking forward to
this new part of the mission. In what seemed
like just a few days, they had been catapulted
three years into the future, arrived in a world
now decimated by nuclear war, and plagued
with zombies. In Colonel Ryder Mountjoy's
mind, they were adjusting pretty well
considering that almost everyone and
everything, including their friends, families,

and prior lives were nothing but a distant memory

Achilles ventured forward past the rescue swimmer and put on a headset to speak to the pilot. He overheard the radio call letting the ship know that they were inbound and should be wheels down within half an hour. Both the pilots and the rest of the crew had been pretty great and right on time picking the team up, and the food was fantastic. There is nothing like fresh sandwiches when you have been running for your life for a few days. The pilot, whose call sign was Nighthawk 27, looked back and gave Achilles a wink, then handed him a cup of coffee from the green thermos that he was using. He spent a few moments telling Achilles why the pick up at the landing zone had been delayed, and that the Captain of the Chung Hoon had just about hung the maintenance crew from the yardarm to get them motivated to get the bird in the air ASAP.

That gave Achilles the opening to get the rundown on "The Old Man." As the pilot started to describe the ship's Captain, it made Achilles laugh a little to himself, and also wonder what the thing was with military pilots always talking like they were from Texas. The pilot went on to describe the Captain. "Captain Josiah Tripp Teeple". He's soft-spoken but has a little bit of a temper. It was his idea to take most of the crew's families with the sailors before the outbreak made it to Pearl Harbor. The brass in the Navy threatened to court martial him, but the boys and girls and the crew saw it as heroic. He kept the crew safe, and also acts like a grandfather to each and every child on the ship. The fact that we are still afloat and have kept it together is a sure sign that the Skipper is good at his job." He went on to tell Achilles that more info would be available once they got under way.

Achilles rejoined the rest of the team, since they were just a few moments from landing on the back of the guided missile cruiser. Everyone had headsets on and took heed to buckle up as they were told that Nighthawk would have to plant the bird on the back of the ship. The USS Chung Hoon (DDG-93) was a fairly newer Aegis Class Destroyer. According to the rescue swimmer, Mack, it had been named after a Rear Admiral that received the Navy Cross and the Silver Star. Mack told them to hold on tight since the deck was actually designed for SH-60 Seahawk Helicopters. The reason the Osprey was onboard was because it had longer range, and they had run out of patches ("replacement parts") for the helos since the fleet, or what was left of it, had scattered to the winds. He went on to tell them that once they were refueled and refit that they would have three functioning aircraft.

Just as the pilot and the swimmer had told them, they touched down with the amount of force that would've loosened the gums of anyone with bad teeth. Nighthawk came across the internal communication system and told them, "Thank you for Flying Air Navy, please feel free to take your belongings on the way out." The team could see that this was getting the best of their own resident pilot and now Purple Heart recipient Hollywood. Also, they noticed how gingerly he was walking due to the shot in the ass that he had taken a day and a half before the rendezvous with the Osprey.

The ramp was down and they could see the team of refuelers, mechanics, and armament workers going to town on the aircraft. They looked like flies on shit; they were moving, the ship was moving and swaying a little, and they acted like it didn't bother them whatsoever. On cue, there was the Skipper standing next to the door (or as they called it the hatch). He had a gargantuan of a man standing next to him. Achilles walked up, dropped his bag and saluted, not because he had to since they were the same rank, but that is what you do when you come into someone else's house in the military. Captain Teeple returned his salute, offered Achilles a handshake, then told Achilles and the team to follow "Big Joe" and that he would be with them in a little while. The Skipper needed to talk to the pilots and crew and make sure his boys were all good to go prior to the briefing that he had prepared for the team.

Big Joe was true to his name. He grabbed Achilles' hand and nearly broke it shaking it. Moon and Opie were talking in hushed tones, and Meat asked what the deal was. It was a bit windy so no one was privy to the conversation that the three were having. Opie said, "I am pretty sure that Big Joe is 'Beefcake.'" Beefcake was a former Air Force Para-Rescue guy who had gotten out and become a wrestler. The last they'd heard, he was in Japan doing the Pro Wrestling circuit. Meat had to agree, Big Joe was one large sum-bitch if he had ever seen one.

As the team made their way through the belly of the ship, Big Joe used a friendly voice to say things like "Make way, make a hole, Beefcake coming through," and even tousled the hair of a child here and there as they walked through the spaces that made up the deck of the ship. The guy didn't seem to have a mean bone in his body. A few of the kids would jump out around corners and try to scare him, and the gentle giant would tell them not to get in "Beefcake's" way; they would just laugh and run off.

Most of the team had spent at least a little time on a ship during their careers, and this one was like most of them, clean, tidy, and not a thing out of place. For a ship that was still floating, operational, and still working as if it were in the Navy, it was nothing short of impressive since it was three years post-apocalypse. Big Joe escorted them to a room, or as the Navy called it, a space. It was mostly plain except for a large dry erase board and seats that looked like they were from a theatre. He told the team that there would be coffee and something to eat in a little while, and that the Skipper would be in before they knew it. They took the time to put their gear down, sit down and stretch out.

Achilles looked around and could already see that the younger Brown was going to toss his cookies at any time. He asked Big Joe for a trashcan, and passed it over. Big Brown was laughing at this, called his son a wuss, and then started to say things like "pork chop dipped in an ashtray," "mmmm, Copenhagen spit is great to drink," and then the rest of the team started in. Achilles laughed as did they all. It was Big Joe that put them all over the edge and into hysterics when he said, "Damn, boy, spill those guts before I make you eat an ass sandwich." That was it, Little Brown retched up everything he had in his stomach, Opie then puked; he sheepishly explained that he was a sympathy puker, and Big Joe turned on the exhaust fan with a shake of his head.

The laughing went on for a little while. There was a lot of backslapping and a general warming up to Big Joe. Achilles thought to himself, "It's always good to laugh, you can make yourself and those around you feel better, and it helps to take the edge of the seriousness of the mission."

That's when Moon spoke up. "Hey Big Joe, I noticed that you don't have any rank on your uniform, and to be honest, Opie and I both know who you are. Could you oblige us with how you ended up on a naval ship after the end of days?"

"Oh hell, I thought I was going to get away without having to answer that to anyone," Big Joe responded. "When all the shit went down with the Koreans, I was doing house shows in Japan. I had gotten real into the oriental women, and decided that I wasn't going to ever go back to the States. Hell, I was as big as Hogan in his heyday, but it was in Japan. I had been doing house shows, exhibition sumo matches, even played a little basketball with the national team in Japan. I was on all the talk shows, and the women were out of this world. I was on my boat with a few women when Japan decided to nuke the Koreans. When the EMP ("Electro Magnetic Pulse") ripped through the Pacific, my boat was disabled, and I lost my passengers overboard. I used my training from the USAF (United States Air Force) and it was all I could do to make it. After around a month, here comes the Chung Hoon. They were sailing up and down the coast of Japan and China looking for survivors. The Skipper picked me up, told me he was a huge fan of wrestling, and made me his bodyguard.

That was over three years ago, and this is my home now."

Opie and Moon looked almost star struck, which led to the opening for Achilles. "Big Joe, what did you do in the Air Force?"

Big Joe laughed and said, "Nothing very important. I was just an Airman like everyone else, decided that I needed to be patriotic, and joined up after college. I did my six and went on my way to become Beefcake."

"Okay, well Airman, since you are on a Naval vessel, do you care to tell me what you did as 'just' an Airman?" That was Meat's response, since it seemed that Big Joe was dancing around the subject.

"All right Sir, I just don't like all the fuss about myself. I was a PJ (Para-Jumper), loved all the adventure stuff, just thought that the fun would take a toll on my body so that's why I left when I did."

"PJ?" said Achilles. "That is *all* you were? You have to say that with more pride, Airman, that is one hard school, and you should be damn proud of yourself."

Big Joe was beaming. You could tell that he didn't like to talk about himself, and that the whole wrestling thing had made him larger than life, but after it was all said and done he was an honest, whole-hearted, and genuine person. Those are the types that make it in the Special Operations community. Sure, there are the Type A personalities, but the quiet, consummate professionals are the ones that keep it going, and also make it happen on a daily basis.

Chapter 2

The Skipper

The team was sitting with Big Joe, and the smell of a cigar was getting stronger by the moment. Big Joe let them know, "The Skipper is inbound, always has the pipe going when he is inside. He is a good man, and please don't think he expects to be treated like a god." That part was interesting to hear. Some of the Captains from the Navy had acted like modern day Gods while they were in command of ships in the old days. The ship was their domain, and many took advantage of this, but not Skip Teeple. He was a good Skipper, loved his boys, their families, and the ship. And with that, they all loved him back.

The Skipper came into the room and everyone sat upright like they should when someone who is in charge of a situation walks into a room. He said "At ease," and went to the front of the room. Big Joe got up and walked up beside him, then after a few quiet words from the Skipper pulled down the screen to put the display on.

The Skipper cleared his throat and began. "Gentlemen, trust me when I say we are going to get you where you need to be. I will answer all of your questions as we go through the briefing. Our route will take us about a month; we need to go by Pearl and do a recon for the Command at Cheyenne, see if we can do anything there, then off to our secret base. Don't worry, I will tell you about it during our briefing. Then we'll get you guys within the drop site. We have done a few recons of the area, and think that we can get you guys close to where the suspected site is located." This got the nods of the men, and with that the Skipper asked if there were any questions before he started.

Achilles said, "Skipper, can you give us a rundown of how you guys got here, what you experienced, and what you know about the

Pacific Rim in the brief?"

"No worries," said the Skipper, "it's all part of this briefing." He then turned on the PowerPoint and started with what they had been through. "The day before the emergency meeting at the U.N., we had been out on a seven hour Tiger cruise. For those of you that don't know what that is, we had the families on board, had left Pearl, and were taking everyone out and doing some demonstrations. We were with a carrier called the Reagan, a sub named the Alabama, and a few support ships. To make a long story short, there had been an underwater quake in the Pacific, and most of the islands in Hawaii had been bombarded by Tsunami waves. It wasn't too bad, we took a few bumps while out to sea, but being on the leeward side of the islands we only had a few 15 to 20 foot rogue waves. This turned our world at sea a little upside down. The Pacific Fleet Commander had advised all of our ships to stay out to sea and make do, that way we wouldn't have to deal with, or be in the way of the clean-up on the islands. By noon the next day, due to the rapid spread of the zombie virus, the ICBM's had been launched, passed each other in flight, and there was nuclear fallout and destruction in over 98% of the habitable land masses in the world. We were essentially on our own with the Reagan for a week before we had coms with the Command at Cheyenne. From there on out, Satcom (Satellite Communication), and everything else was in shambles. We were only in communication with the rest of the fleet sporadically and with Command for around six hours a day. There has been no contact from the international space station. They seem to have fallen off the grid as soon as NASA went down. There is some speculation that they used the emergency re-entry capsules, but there would be no one to pick them up. We've picked up survivors, and have been making regular recons, rescues and stops when it is safe. The base we use is on Midway, it is an old World War II base that we've always kept up. Without it, we would be out of supplies. We have put together a few Seals and some recruits that always wanted to do that gung ho shit; they have been going ashore on some of the islands on supply runs and what not. I am a little nervous about what they want me to do to help you guys get where you need to be, but I don't have to get the ship close to let you get on with your mission. We have a secure site near the DMZ that was a CIA base, hell, I didn't even know that it existed. There is a skeleton crew there, and they have some gear and transportation for you to use while searching for this cure or whatever else you guys can find. I will speak offline with you, Achilles, about what we know. I know that you all have clearances, but I like to keep things a little old school: I brief your CO, your CO briefs you and so on. This will be a little bit of a lengthy trip, so make yourselves at home. We have most anything that you need here on the ship, so please use the time to get cleaned up, gear changed, weapons cleaned." Here he paused and turned to Woody. "And get that ass wound checked out by the Doc we have on board here, Chief."

With that the Skipper left. Big Joe stayed back to show the team to their berthing quarters, and said he would take Hollywood to see the Doctor. On the way through the halls they passed the nerve center of the ship, the operations center. Achilles had been on ships before, and this one had the usual buzz of activity. The Skipper was there in the thick of things. He waved Achilles inside while Big Joe led the rest of the team to their berth.

The Skipper and Achilles went to a desk in the back, or what you would consider a desk in the ship. There was a nameplate and a computer terminal. The Skipper said, "I prefer to work off of the bridge, but I have a desk down here for when we were doing maneuvers in the Gulf during the conflict. We have a few hours until we can contact Cheyenne. You need to know that I am not the most popular man with the Command. I disobeyed a direct order from the President to evacuate the ship, but over the past few years they now think that I am a rogue hero for keeping some part of humanity alive. I couldn't ask the sailors aboard this ship to leave their young ones and families to try to survive on the islands. We have stayed alive by being careful, and to be honest, our having to take you guys across the Pacific twice is not the safest thing for this crew."

Achilles nodded gravely. "Skipper, I understand what you are saying. Hell, until about two weeks ago we never even knew what was going on. We are part of a mission that began prior to this even going down. We came to know about this three years after it happened. I am not too sure what they have briefed you on, and when we get the Command on the horn, I will ask them to bring you up to speed. We just are doing what we are told, we follow orders like every soldier, sailor, marine, airman, and government employee is supposed to do. I actually think what you did is heroic, Sir."

"The base on Wake Colonel is really a miracle," the Skipper said with a smile. "I am not sure how much money that the government sank into the place, but we would never have made it if the President hadn't survived and took up residence there. The entire island is free of infection; they didn't get hit by anything more than a few storms. With such a small population, and the fact that there are defenses there beyond even my speculation, they are really one of the last hopes that we have. Alaska is the same. Any small islands off of the coasts around the world are hoped to be similar refuges. The mainlands are full of the walking dead as you have experienced. We just hope that we can keep restocking. Eventually, if your mission is a success, maybe we can have somewhat of a return to our lives. Sure, we will never in our lifetimes be able to go back to the hustle and bustle of corporate America, but at least maybe we can eradicate the dead from more places and these dead or zombies will just die off."

While the Skipper and Achilles were talking, Big Joe took Hollywood to the infirmary. There were not too many people there, a few kids with coughs or colds, a sailor with a burn from something that happened on the ship, and a guy that could only be described as looking like a dwarf from Middle Earth. He wasn't that short, but his features looked strikingly similar to a character from that movie about the Ring.

"Oh, hey there," said the Doctor. "My name is Dickie Lyons. I was a Nurse Practitioner prior to this. I see you have a bit of blood on your posterior. Come right in and sit down." Hollywood shook the Doc's hand, and took a seat on the gurney that was nearest to him.

"You said Lyons, where are you from, Doc?" Hollywood asked curiously. Opie's last name was Lyons.

"Oh, I am from Indianapolis, but was on Oahu when it all happened. I was doing a rotation at Pearl, and had luckily been aboard this ship. It was a volunteer thing, but I just am lucky as hell to have been at sea with this crew. Their doctor was sick when they went on the Tiger cruise, and I volunteered to take his place since I had never been on a ship."

That got Woody thinking. Lyons, both from Indianapolis, and they were big guys, maybe they were related? He would talk to Opie about it.

The Doc then had Woody take off his pants and put on a robe. Unbeknownst to Woody, Big Joe was recording the whole thing. The Doc had told Joe that he was going to screw with this guy, and that he should film it for his guests. He knew what a good kick soldiers got out of each other's embarrassing moments.

"Ok young man, looks like your friend got the bullet out. There is a clean wound, with just a little bit of infection. I am going to sterilize it and then clean it out. I will dress it with a few stitches, and then give you a shot of penicillin. I need to also check your prostate; just to make sure that nothing is messed up on the inside."

While this was going on, Moon snuck in. Big Joe had let him in on what was going on, and the Doc was all about the fun.

Hollywood bent over the exam table, the Doc put gloves on both hands, lubed up one finger, then inserted it into Woody's anus. Being a pilot, Woody was used to the yearly exam, and he was just happy that the Doc had small hands. It is one of those things that every pilot would laugh after, making jokes about "call me later" and such. As the Doc inserted his finger, Woody groaned, and the Doc told him to be calm. At that point, Moon, who was hiding, came in and put his hand on Woody's other shoulder. Woody gave an almost girlish scream and launched up onto the exam table. As it would later be explained, Woody thought he was getting raped by a male nurse. With that, the exam was over, he got a clean bill of health, and was told that the stitches would be removed in a few days. Moon was still laughing hysterically in the corner, leaning on Big Joe who was in no better shape.

The team gathered in their berth, learned the layout of the ship from Big Joe along with the chow schedule, where the latrines were located (since there was no longer a place referred to as Officer Country), and the schedule that the ship operated on. Achilles and the team were called up to the deck to have coffee with the Skipper. They all sat about and reflected on the beautiful sunset, and got ready to speak to Cheyenne on the upcoming conference call.

Chapter 3

Calling Cheyenne

The team gathered at the big screen in the belly of the ship. This place was what was known as Combat. This was the nerve center of the newer ships in the Navy's fleet. There was a big screen, and the Captain could actually control the ship and all of the systems from this section. All of the vital systems and people who control them work there. Since there wasn't really a threat from other ships, and there weren't any pirates that could take over the Chung Hoon, they were able to clear it out except for the team, Big Joe, the Skipper, and the Doctor.

Right at 6 p.m. Pacific Time, Cheyenne came online. It was good for the team to see Honcho (the Secretary of Defense), Eagle (the President), and a few other people from the fortified bunker that the leaders of the United States now resided in. The team and everyone else came right to the position of attention and executed flawless salutes to their leadership.

The world might not be what it once was, and the United States was basically a place where there was little to no population, but military customs and courtesy were still active with this group.

The President told them, "As you were." This was basically telling them to sit down and to dispense with all of the courtesy, that way he could get to the point and be able to use the brief time that was given to them to its max potential. The first thing that was brought up on the screen was the graphic of South Korea. The president told them that they would brief daily during the voyage, and that every last bit of ammunition and provisions, "What little it was," would be available to the team while they were on the ground during the actual operation.

The President went on. "The first thing is that we will actually be taking you up the West Coast of the Korean Peninsula. This will enable the HALO (High Altitude Low Opening) jump to keep you as covert as possible. The situation there is pretty bleak. As far as we can tell, there are a large amount of runners. The people on the ground were so badly affected by the virus that the ones that weren't decimated by the nuclear blasts, well, they are just bad news. Can

I see by a show of hands who has spent time in Korea?" Almost the entire team had been there, and with exception to Little Brown, even the Skipper and Big Joe had been there.

"A little back-story. Most of our U.S. forces had been taken south of Seoul prior to 2005. This was an agreement with the South Korean government. Since then we have been operating some of the previous black ops out of a few places that used to be part of our installations. To be exact, there was an airfield that was just south of a base called Camp Stanley. It was a very tactical base due to its being on the side of a mountain. The reason we never really abandoned it is because we have a hanger inside of the mountain. This houses the element of the CIA that we still have there. They are in contact a couple of hours a day, and they will be your support that will get you transportation to the north. The second thing that is great about this location, Uijongbu, is that the city that is near it had a train station. We know that these tracks run all the way to the DMZ (Demilitarized Zone), and since we think that the facility is in what the North Koreans called Freedom City, well, it is just a hop, skip, and a jump across the border.

Third, there is a hardened hanger that is right back south of the DMZ at Camp Bonnefest. As a few of you know, that is where they would supposedly stand alone if the conflict came back into being. There is a Command and Control Bunker there, and we actually still have a skeleton crew at that location. If you can believe it, the Commander of the 2nd Infantry Division and his staff of CIA agents are still there. They have one Chinook that is ready to go, and that is where you will exfil. Hollywood, can you fly the MH-47?"

Woody acknowledged that he had spent some time in the aircraft, and he would have no issues getting them out via this mode of transportation.

"After you men exfil, you will then link up with the Chung Hoon off of the East Coast. At that point, you will sail for Washington State, and link up with your ride back to Cheyenne. This is the part of the plan still in the works, but we have a Commander at Fort Richardson that says with the help of a Crab boat. He can get you guys a few vehicles to get back this way.

"Are there any questions at this time?"

The group all stated that they were good to go, and then the President told them that they would reconvene the next day at the same time. Achilles and the Skipper remained after the rest of the team left Combat and continued to speak with the President and his staff. They spoke for a little while about logistics and personnel. The main part of the conversation was Achilles getting permission to add Big Joe to the team.

"Sir, we could use this guy. He is first of all a mountain of a man, and secondly, well, he is a Para Rescue guy. This Airman needs no training, and I know the Skipper trusts him, and if he can, well Sir, so can we."

The President turned it over to Honcho. "I see what you are saying Achilles, and if Captain Teeple is in agreement, then he is yours. The sheer fact that he knows the equipment and how to HALO is just the icing on the top of the cake. I can see that this brings the team to eight, that works well, that way there are two fire teams, or at least a breach and a support by fire team when talking about conventional warfare."

That left it on the Skipper, he had his hand on his chin and seemed to be contemplating the entire situation. He took a moment to light his cigar. His response seemed to be clear, well thought, and contemplated. "Sir, I agree with your and Achilles' assessment. Joe is a good man, most of the crew think of him as their uncle, and the kids love him to death. I agree also that this mission is bigger than my ship and or its crew. I will leave it in the hands of Achilles to speak to Joe, and I think that we should let Big Joe be part of this decision. It's his life, and he is trying to survive like the rest of us. As I have already said, I think he will go with the team, he is very patriotic, and as you have both stated, he would be a great benefit to this mission."

This ended the briefing, and the President signed off. The Skipper and Achilles spoke about who should bring it up to Big Joe. They agreed that Achilles should do it. That way Big Joe wouldn't feel obligated to be part of this mission just because the Skipper requested him to do it.

Achilles and the Skipper went their separate ways, but they agreed to meet back in an hour in the Captain's mess (where the Captain and officers normally would eat), and the Skipper went on his way toward the Bridge.

Achilles walked back to their space to speak to the team. He knew they would be all for Big Joe being a part of it; as he approached he heard the laughter of the team. It was good for them to have this downtime and to be a little loose around each other. They would need it, the rest would refresh them all, and the plain fact was right in front of him. Despite what they had already faced, they would be in for the fight of their lives while on the ground in Korea.

He entered the room, and found that they were watching the video of the examination of Woody's prostate. He couldn't help but laugh hysterically with the rest of the team. Big Joe was there, and his laughter was that of nothing short of a horn. Moon was playing it in slow motion, and the look on Woody's face was nothing short of priceless. If they were in the conventional Army at this point and someone released this video, heads would roll. The press would tear this up as a sort of hazing. The great thing about the apocalypse was that they didn't have to worry about that anymore.

Achilles stepped in front of the projector, looked to the team and Big Joe, and told them he needed a few moments of pure seriousness. "Big Joe, I have a question for you and the rest of the team. After speaking to Honcho and Eagle, we have concluded that you would be a great asset to our team, how do you feel about joining us?"

At that point Big Joe stopped him by standing up. "Sir, I have loved my time on this ship, to be honest it has become my home. It would kill me if any of these children suffered the same fate as the people who went through the end of days. We've got to stop this virus, or find a cure. If you will have me, I would like to be part of the team."

That did it. Achilles looked around at the rest of the team, and they all nodded in agreement. He stepped forward and they all shook hands with Big Joe. From now on he would use his code name, and they all knew it would be Beefcake.

Achilles and the team spent the next hour or so going over the op. They would use decks of the ship to practice dry fire, even room clearing and getting Stewy set up in a lab. They would use the rest of the cruise to Midway to practice using coms, movement techniques, and general preparation for the operation. They stored the weapons, at least the long range ones, and just kept side arms on themselves. They might be on a secure ship but they were all to the point of not being too careful. They would have to go through the weapons locker on the ship and get Big Joe and the Browns set up with matching calibers and equipment as the rest of the team. They would set up two fire teams to space out the PADS and also the rest of the loads. Hopefully they would be able to get more gear and also better preparation while on Midway.

They got up and moved as a team to the Captain's Mess. This was when Moon realized he had not thought to speak to Opie about Lyons. Opie was in the back of the group, and when Moon saw Dickie Lyons he wasn't sure how Opie would react. The Skipper and Dickie were seated at the table, and when Achilles and the rest of the team came in Opie stopped dead in his tracks.

"Dick, how the hell are you here?"

Both men broke into tears and nearly knocked the others out of the way as they hugged. Dickie spent the next little while going over how he made it to the ship and how he had become part of the crew. He just couldn't believe that his little brother was still alive. Who would have thought it, brothers reunited thousands of miles away from home, on a ship, and during the apocalypse no less.

They spent the next few hours all telling old war stories, some funny, some heart wrenching, and they bonded like tight knit units usually do. The Skipper excused himself to check on the crew, and on his way out stopped and placed a hand on Big Joe's shoulder. "I am very proud of you, young man. I don't want to lose you, but I know that you were placed here by a higher power to be on this team." The two shook hands warmly and the Skipper left.

Chapter 4

En Route to Midway

The trip to Midway took around twenty-five days to accomplish. They had to change course a few times to avoid the acid and toxic rain systems caused by nuclear fallout. During that time the team was able to gel as a close knit unit. Hollywood was healed from the wound to his posterior, and they had cross loaded and made a list of supplies that they would need to requisition while they were at port. The best part of the time for Achilles was finally getting to heal up the wounded shoulder that he had said was good to go. Every time he raised his weapon, it hurt, and climbing and moving hurt. All in all this had been a much needed time of rest for him and his team.

The day that they were going to make port, the conference call with Cheyenne was upbeat. The supplies that the team had requested was gathered and waiting on them in port. Also, there was the possibility that they might get to the mission quicker. They had a C-130 Hercules cargo plane that could get them there much faster; the only problem was going to be getting the C-130 back after the drop. Since there were no more refuelers flying, this made for that being more a plan B than a plan A. The Browns were now trained up on the drop, and with the practice and training that they had on the ship, and hopefully two to three jumps while on Midway, it would make it more of a sure thing they could count on. If they were to pull this off and insert as a team without being detected, it would be a miracle.

The supply locker on the ship worked out well. They were able to make sure the entire team had M-4's, but the Browns and Big Joe would all have different side arms for the time being. Big Brown would not come off of his 8 inch .44 Smith and Wesson Magnum hand cannon that he had strapped to his side. That was not a big deal to Achilles, many a man had their favorite gun, and this one was no different.

The Skipper had requested that Achilles join him on the bridge, and that was a welcome relief from the monotonous days that they had spent on the ship. Sure, it was great to be able to come together as a team, but outside of training there was only so much you could do. There was a movie played every night, and it seemed that the collection on board was quite extensive, but they still seemed to play some of the same movies night in and night out.

The food was good on board, and the fact that they would all probably eat canned goods for the foreseeable future was a whole other issue that they would have to live with. At least there was running water and toilet paper where they were headed. That was one thing that Achilles would hate to have to go without: toilet paper. He wasn't sure that life was worth living if you had to use leaves the entire time, it was the one comfort item that most soldiers always made sure that they had with them.

On the bridge the Skipper was waiting. As usual he was smoking a pipe. Achilles thought it was a little bit nostalgic, a Skipper smoking a pipe on a ship, if that wasn't a stereotype then there wasn't one out there. The Skipper turned and looked at Achilles. He had a smile on his face but the team leader could tell that there was an issue.

"Col. How is our boy doing with the team?"

Achilles responded and told him that Big Joe was fitting in just fine, and that the training was going as well as could be expected. The Browns were adjusting well, and even the Doc was managing to keep up during the physical training sessions. "Sir," Achilles asked. "How is everything looking for our few days on Terra Firma?" And that was the needle in the haystack, the issue that had been bothering the Skipper. He opened a door that led out to the side of the bridge. It was a balcony of sorts, and was where the Skipper would normally be found if it were nice out.

"The problem is, Achilles, we have no clue. Cheyenne lost coms with them three days ago, and I haven't been able to get in contact for four days. We haven't said anything to alert you or your team yet, but we may have to go in and take some stuff by force. Or, they could just be having some sort of issue with the radio and communications array, who knows, we have to deal with this all of the time. I know it's not on our end, I spoke to Cheyenne earlier. I just hope that when we get there, we can get some fuel, food, and other supplies and get back out to sea. This is my domain, and I don't like to put my crew into too much danger. The other problem is the insertion. I know the boys have been trying to crunch the numbers, and hell, they have already done the flight a few times. If we cannot get you and your team there by C-130, we may have to use the Osprey. I really don't want to lose my only operational aircraft on a one-way mission!"

The Skipper went on to discuss the mission details, flight path, range, wind conditions, and favorable options. "If we get to Midway, and the place is a ghost town, or if it is overrun by those zombies, we are up shit creek without a paddle. And if that happens, you guys may have to row to Korea."

Achilles knew that the Skipper can't bitch down, and at least when he was talking to him it was a lateral bitching order. It is one of those things that they refer to as the "Burden of Command," you can really only blame yourself and those above you when stuff ends up FUBAR, and when that happens, you just have to make it work.

The Skipper told Achilles that they would try to get coms up and working, and that if there was any change that they would let him know. The decision was made to take the Osprey up and try to get a visual of the situation in Midway, that way they could try to get some Intel on the situation prior to the ship making port to avoid being unprepared. That was a sound plan, and Achilles offered up Hollywood to go with the flight crew. That way they could concentrate on flying and communications while Woody could try to get a good look at the situation.

That made it a go mission. They would take off in the morning, and the ship and crew would be a good twelve hours out from docking at Midway. They could do the recon and be back on deck in less than three hours of flight time. The aircraft was good to go, the crew was briefed, and even the weather looked like it would be of no concern. All in all, this was the safest thing to do. Achilles was already formulating a plan to get the supplies that they would need if something very bad had happened to the base.

Chapter 5

Midway

As the Osprey left the deck, most of the crew seemed to be on edge. The people really wanted to get off of the boat and feel a little bit of Terra Firma. That's the way it always is with being on a ship.

Achilles was in the Combat Nerve Center of the ship with the Skipper. It had been a fruitful past couple of hours. The Reagan had made contact with the Chung Hoon, and they would be able to meet and help out with the operation. The last time the Skipper had heard from the Reagan, they were outside of New Zealand and were assessing smaller islands in the Pacific for survivors and a place to start the world free of the infection. With them heading to the Sea of China, there would be a place for the Osprey to land and refuel. They were also in pretty good shape. Their skipper had done about the same thing as the Chung Hoon's

Skipper, so they still had operational planes and helos that could help the operation if need be. The second bit of good news was the fact that most of Seal Team 5 was on the Reagan. Well, it really wasn't the actual team, but a few members and some volunteers that had been battle hardened on scavenging missions. They would be able to help out if the mission went way wrong. That part at least made Achilles feel a little better. The fact that there were some Special Operation soldiers still alive and doing their jobs made him feel good.

During the time the recon flight was going on, the team prepped on the ship for an assault on the base. Their plan was full of contingencies because the crew of the ship needed supplies, and without them it would be a one way trip for the ship. Achilles knew that the Skipper wouldn't let that happen, and for their mission to be a go there could possibly be a little give and take. He didn't blame the Skipper, hell, if he had a positive known fact that his parents and daughter were alive, he would be off getting them right now. He wasn't the only person in the team thinking about things like this. They had all come to grips with the fact that they knew it was almost impossible for their loved ones to be alive. They just didn't talk about it.

The Osprey had been airborne and on their recon for about an hour, and the Seeker team was still getting prepped just in case they had to make ready for an assault mission. Achilles and the Skipper were planning how they could get a team in and out if the shit had hit the proverbial fan at the base. They were all a little on edge. A mission would involve many lives, the possible loss of same, and they might lose supplies, ammunition, and time. These three things were all pretty key at this point. They would need everything that they already had at their disposal. It was looking pretty grim, and Achilles could feel it all throughout the ship.

It was all for nothing. The Osprey crew and Woody called back and reported in that the base was secure and good to go. They had a storm come through and the base's antennae array had been knocked offline. Woody had spoken to the command structure at the base, and they were making ready for the Chung Hoon to make port. They also relayed that they would hear everything that was being broadcast their way, they just couldn't transmit. This was

45

a good thing, because Woody knew that Moon could probably get the place up and operational with a pair of pliers, duct tape, and a roll of safety wire.

The rest of the twelve hour voyage was pretty boring. Achilles and the Skipper were on the bridge going over a list of supplies with a few of the naval officers, and Big Joe and the Browns were staying together. This was a good thing since the three of them were going to be the support by fire position. They would be the backup to the assault team, and with both of the Browns being crack shots, that would leave another assaulter to be with the team and Stewy while they entered the compound. The odds were looking better and better and if, God willing, things went well, they would be in and out of Midway, en-route to Korea, and hopefully mission complete outside of a week or so.

The ship made port, or rather they set anchor just inside of port right before dusk. The Skipper explained about the twenty-four hour quarantine, and that they would be able to disembark and get their supplies the next day. He laughed about the quarantine period: If the ship had been to sea, then how the hell would there be anyone infected on the ship? This was a known fact, but it was protocol. Dickie Lyons, who had spent much of the journey with Opie, had a report ready and was sending it to the surgeon on the base. This was basically a rundown of the crew, known illnesses, and a list of those who would be able to get off of the ship. Not all of the families were allowed off, and just a handful of the sailors were allowed to get off of the ship. The Skipper knew that they hated this, but at this point everyone knew that life was a fragile thing, and it had become accepted in the last three years. They rotated every time they came back through, and they generally got off of the ship every ninety or so days for twelve hours.

The team was pretty astonished by the port. There were military ships, naval vessels, and a handful of civilian yachts that were anchored or ported on this remote piece of real estate. Big Joe told them that just about every cruise they would find a boat adrift, go aboard, clear it, and bring the survivors back here. The base itself looked like a functioning town, well, except for the 16 foot concrete and concertina wire wall that separated the base from the rest of the island. He explained how the wall ran into the ocean for a half of a mile, and that there were mines underwater just in case the zombies could walk and not drown. They hadn't had any come through the water, but it was a just in case scenario. So the team settled down to do what every soldier had done for centuries upon centuries: hurry up and wait.

Opie was damn proud of his older brother; he even acted like a damn sailor. The siblings, who had joked about fighting over the military in the past, were now both working for the military in an attempt to stay alive. They had come to grips with the fact that they were the only two left of their family, and this bond would be hard to break. Achilles was sure that on the return trip Dickie would be going with them to Cheyenne. He could never ask Opie to leave his brother behind, because if he were to find any of his family, they would go everywhere with him. The one thing that Achilles had spoken to Opie offline about was the fact that Dickie would have to stay on the ship during the Korea mission, and Opie said he knew and appreciated the boss' blessing on Dickie going with them back to Cheyenne.

Since this was at one time a top secret base used by the CIA, there was no way that the Chung Hoon could fit into the port, so the team would be taking Zodiacs to the base. The Skipper would be remaining on the ship. He told the team that they had twenty-four hours in port, and the Chung Hoon would be pulling up anchor and departing ASAP after that. This wasn't a big deal. the team was basically going straight to the armory, Moon was going to help with the communications array, and then they would get back shipside afterwards anyway.

Moon and Meat left when they got to the dock. Achilles and the rest of the team followed a classic example of a company man to the Armory. He was decked out in dessert boots, khaki 511 pants, a vest, and a pair of the biggest Aviator sunglasses that Achilles had ever seen on a human. He told them his name was Smith, and the team members laughed. "They are all named Smith," is what Achilles thought, and since the world had ended why didn't they use their own names for the love of God. Smith went on to explain on the walk over to the Armory that the island was pretty much devoid of life, this wasn't Midway proper anyway, just an outlying island that they had used since the height of the Cold War in the 1960's.

On the way over, Smith was joined by another company man named Jones. He was a bit more friendly, and even recognized Achilles. "Excuse me sir, but weren't you in Delta? I think we may have met in the 'Stan (Afghanistan)?"

Achilles told him that he had been around, but wouldn't acknowledge that he had been part of the elite unit without someone showing the proper documentation. "Old habits die hard," is all that he said to Jones, and they both laughed a little.

Jones and Smith told them a little more about the base, and even joked that they were lucky that they had been here for a debrief when the shit had went down.

Opie went on to the Armory with the Browns, Woody, and Big Joe. Stewy and Achilles went with Jones and Smith to see the commander of the base. This was probably going to be another classic dick measuring contest that most of the company men always were part of. For those that don't know, that is basically to see who the person with the most pull is. To their surprise, it was nothing of the sort.

The man in charge was named Morgan. They weren't sure if it was his first name, or a made up last name. The meeting was actually very smooth; they spoke about the mission, the assets that were on the ground outside of Uijongbu, and the fact that there was a lot riding on the mission being a success. Morgan briefed them on the two men that would be waiting on them, Snyder and Rahe, two of his men that had been inserted over a year ago, and the fact that they would be able to get them to the supposed facility with not much of a problem. He gave Achilles all of the data that he had been able to gather from what was left of operational satellite imagery, and went over the schematic of the mountainside bunker at the once used Camp Stanley. When they were done, Jones escorted them back to the dock so that they could return to the ship. Smith would get the rest of the team back to the ship shortly.

The armory rivaled that of the one at Atterbury. Big Joe and the Browns were outfitted and geared up within the hour. They also got the chutes that they would need, and enough supplies that the team would be good to go. Both of the Browns were issued M-24 Sniper rifles, Heckler and Koch suppressed MP-5's,claymores, grenades, packs, night vision goggles, and combat vests. Big Brown was even able to find a leg holster for the hand cannon that he preferred to carry as his backup piece.

They spent the rest of the day getting supplies loaded; the team went back to work on preparation work. It would be a five day cruise to get them into position for the Osprey to launch and get them to the drop point. The next five days would prove very useful in getting the finalities and plan together. Achilles wouldn't let any time go to waste. They would be able to speak to the team on the ground when they were about forty-eight hours out, and that would provide the last bit of detail and mission planning that they would need prior to the insertion.

The USS Chung Hoon set a north by northwest course and said goodbye to the island. It had been great to be on Terra Firma for a day, a day of not having to be worried about getting bitten by a damn zombie. The next part of the journey was where Achilles had placed his worries and concerns; he was prepared to go into battle, and ready to lead his men. They all had performed well, and the only wild card was Big Joe. With what he had already shown and his credentials, it made him appear to be a great fit for the team.

Chapter 6

North by Northwest

Achilles gathered the men, as well as the Skipper, his Chief of the Boat, and the two pilots that would be inserting them. They met in the nerve center of the boat and had a teleconference with the team at Cheyenne. This briefing would happen daily until they were on station in Korea. The good thing was that the team at Cheyenne and the team at Camp Stanley were in contact with one another. The bad thing was that all three couldn't speak to each other at the same time of day. That meant there was a whole lot of information being relayed; hopefully this wouldn't cause an issue.

As they continued on their journey, plans were refined, radios and gear were cross-loaded, checked and re-checked, and preparations were made for the insertion. The two teams would be Alpha and Bravo Teams. There would be the assault team which consisted of Achilles, Meat, Hollywood, Opie, Moon and Dr. Stewy. Bravo Team would be commanded by Big Joe, and he would have Big and Little Brown to cover the insertion and ex-filtration from the site in a support by fire position.

The first teleconference with the two CIA operatives at the bunker was quite interesting. One of the two men, Rahe, was skinny and looked like he had smoked an entire factory full of cigarettes. The second man, Snyder, was as pale as a ghost. They both were full of information, and told Achilles that they were working on the transportation to the North side of the DMZ. The city that supposedly housed no one, and was just there as a way to laugh at the south, still had working electricity. All of the Intel that they had showed that the lights came on and went off on their own.

The data that they had collected prior to the attacks had been extensive. They had known that the North was working on something, and they had great video. Snyder went on to explain that they had thought that this was actually an underground facility that the North Koreans used for spying, experiments, and as a military base. They both had been across and gathered firsthand knowledge of the site, and had a good understanding of what was going on. The bad part was that all of the info was over three years old at this point, and they had been holed up for so long they were both a little on the twitchy side. Achilles brushed this off, and during conversations with Honcho they decided that they would be taking the operatives along with them on the mission. This would be briefed to them by Honcho, and they would follow orders.

The Skipper kept on the course that would get the ship into position, and speculated hopefully that they would make it to the departure site within a week or so. The team was prepped.

The Skipper was really a great person for Achilles to speak with about the burden of command. They spent most of their downtime together, and worked tirelessly on the plan of making this a mission with little to no error.

The week went by rather quickly for the team. If there were no issues, they would be on station pretty quickly. The only problem was getting around the southern tip of South Korea. There was a storm and the Skipper wanted to wait it out in the Sea of China. This made great sense. It had been three years since the bombs had obliterated most of the peninsula, but there were still radioactive issues that made the weather bad and could cause the ship to hit pockets of Acid Rain. The wait only took another twenty-four or so hours, but it seemed like an eternity to the team and the crew of the Chung Hoon.

During the twenty-four hours leading up to the mission, they made the final plans. They would launch from the Sea of China, be airborne for a little over an hour, HALO jump over Camp Stanley at night, link up with the CIA team, then continue the next night after dark. Big Brown would tandem jump with Big Joe, and Little Brown would go with Opie. They were not rated as freefall paratroopers, and a solo combat jump at night into unfamiliar territory would not be safe. The best thing that they had going was that Woody had been stationed at an airfield south of Seoul called K-16. It had been a few years, but he had actually drunk beer at Camp Stanley. This gave him and the team a good knowledge of where to go when they hit the ground.

Camp Stanley was an old Aviation base north of Seoul. It was built on the side of a mountain, which is what they would aim for.

Camp Stanley was at one time an ammunition bunker that had been converted when the U.S. turned the base back over to the South Koreans in the late 2000's. There was a 200 by 200 foot pad that could be used for helicopters, and was a great place for them to land. There were no power lines in the way, so that wasn't a concern for the jumpers.

The day of the mission came and the team was ready to go. The Osprey was prepped, and the flight crew was ready to get it going. The Skipper launched a drone and was able to get real time info of the area around the base. As the team and Woody watched, they were all in awe of the destruction that had fallen upon the base and the surrounding area. You could tell that there were buildings at one time, but the entire area looked as if God himself had just swept his hand across the board and cleared it. During the sweep by the drone, there were no zombies spotted anywhere. Achilles had the drone fly all the way up to the DMZ and they didn't see a single structure that had survived the nuclear devastation. This area was full of life at one time, but now it looked like a desert.

Four hours prior to the takeoff, the team was eating and starting the backwards preparations that all military teams go through prior to time on target. Satellites that still functioned were moved into position over the peninsula so the team would have communications with Cheyenne for sixteen hours a day. Opie and Dickie said their goodbyes to one another, and it almost brought a tear to the eye of some of the other team members. Achilles had a talk with Opie to make sure that he was good to go, and without a doubt the soldier was ready for action. If all went well, in under seventy-two hours they would all be back on the ship and sailing back to the once United States of America.

The Osprey would actually drop the team from 36,000 feet over Stanley. They would then open their chutes at 2000 feet and do their best to hit the target. This would be hard for the team, and even harder for the two tandem jumpers. Big Joe didn't seem to be the least bit concerned with having Big Brown attached to him. The team on the ground would mark the landing zone with IR (Infra-Red) chemical lights to guide them in. Once on the ground they would seek shelter in the bunker and then get on with the mission from there.

If someone were to get blown off course or miss the LZ, they would have to make their way to the bunker. They all had their trackers on, and knew where they would go. There wouldn't be the fog of battle to contend with, and with nothing moving on the ground, this should be dangerous, but relatively the easiest part of the mission. At 2300 hours they loaded the plane and they set off on what was hopefully a mission for all of mankind, not just for the sake of the United States of America.

Chapter 7

The Jump

The flight was filled with the usual apprehension and a little bit of butterflies for all of the team. This was one thing that always made Achilles laugh, he had been on hundreds of jumps, and he was nervous each and every time. Both of the Browns had to be scared shitless, they hadn't been on a night time free fall before, and they would be connected to other jumpers. The rest of the team were all rated free fall parachutists, so they would be nervous, but should at least be competent. The wild card would be Stewy. He was a sport free-fall jumper, so he should have no issue, it was just jumping with the goggles on that would be a little bit of a hamper. They all had IR chem lights on their ankles. This was used so that in theory they would be able to follow one another to the drop zone.

The drop zone itself wasn't all that large, and should not become that much of an issue. It was a cool night, and not overly breezy, so those factors were playing in well to the team's hand. At the bottom of the mountain there was an old airfield that was flattened at this point, so that was the backup landing zone. The rally point was at the primary LZ, and there was nothing showing on the drones' fly over that should cause the team much of an issue.

The final preparations were made in the airplane, then the ramp was lowered into the jump position. Achilles could feel the apprehension like sweat coming off of a basketball player. The team all gave the "good to go" signals, and the two tandem teams were hooked up. The light inside the cabin was turned on and illuminated everything in red light. The crew chief gave the one minute signal and everyone edged out to the end of the ramp. The next signal was thirty seconds; their oxygen was flowing and their goggles were all down in the ready position. It seems like a long time to those who are jumping, but actually it flies by.

"GREEN LIGHT, GO, GO, GO!"

And with that they were free falling. The Osprey would continue on course and actually go down to ground level and do three false insertions prior to heading back to the boat. This was standard protocol for most insertions. They were unsure if the Supreme Ruler on the North side was still in control. If he was, he would be watching what was going on in the wasteland of South Korea.

The team was hurtling toward the earth at terminal velocity. They had formed up and would deploy their chutes at 2,000 feet. They had all made their way into the loose ring that free fall teams always formed, and things looked to be going great. Moon actually saw the LZ first and motioned to the rest of the team where to head once they deployed their chutes.

At 2500 feet Achilles gave the signal to spread and they deployed their chutes. He counted and they all deployed. The rest of the drop went well. Everyone but Opie hit the primary LZ, but Opie ended up in a tree 50 feet short. He had caught a thermal cell and mistimed the turn. No harm, no foul. Within moments they were all together, chutes were bundled and they were met by Snyder and Rahe.

The CIA men brought them into the bunker and secured the outside doors. From there they were able to watch the flight of the Osprey on the screen and made contact with Captain Teeple. The Osprey flight was going well, but on their third false insertion they were engaged by a SAM (Surface to Air Missile) just north of the DMZ. They deployed countermeasures and flew back to the coast following NOE (or Nap of the Earth) flight route. This way they stayed low, and were not engaged again.

Snyder and Rahe were hard at work pinpointing the position of the SAM site. This was good and bad: Good because they would be able to locate whoever was controlling it, but bad because that meant there were still North Koreans alive on the other side. This would cause a change in plans for the mission, or what was more commonly referred to as a FRAGO (a fragmentation order or a change in plans during a mission).

This would set the entire time-table back a day or two, and the extraction would now be on call instead of at a set time. Both Captain Teeple and Achilles agreed that speaking with Cheyenne prior to anything else would be a good idea. This had to work, because there were no other teams to complete the mission. This nation was already strapped for resources, and the fact that they had no second option made this the best plan to go from.

The team got some rack time, and Achilles and Meat went over the mission details with Rahe and Snyder. At this point they were both given the same option as the others: what call sign to use. Snyder and Rahe said they were used to this already, and from now on they would be known as Ghost and Smoke. That made Achilles chuckle, as Snyder was one of the palest people that he had ever met and Rahe smelled like a five day old ashtray. Meat brought that up, and Smoke said that he would be smoke free during the mission and that the smell wouldn't be a problem. They would be split between the assault team and the support team.

The next thing was integrating the radio coms that they would use. They had no pad communication, but had an earlier model that synced up without any problem. They spent the next few hours getting Achilles and his second up to speed on what they knew. Kijondong, otherwise known as Peace Village or Propaganda Village, would be the primary place that the team would be heading toward.

"This place is spooky to say the least," Rahe said. "The lights go on automatically. There were supposedly two hundred workers that lived there, but from the U.S. side, we never saw anyone go in or out. It was rumored to be an underground facility which housed the nuclear program and where the advanced testing was done. Every American soldier that was ever stationed at or near the DMZ knew of this place. Soldier of Fortune Magazine had a million dollar standing bounty if anyone could get the flag that flew there into their hands.

The CIA guys went on to explain that they had been tasked with infiltrating the facility prior to the day of reckoning, but when the decision has been made to nuke the peninsula they had had no choice but to take cover and ride out the storm. Since that time, they had to wait out the fallout, and then recon the place until the government could get a team into position to help them to get inside and acquire whatever data was left. It was Snyder's opinion that the Supreme leader was still located there with his little army of faithfuls and whatever zombies he had created.

They would move the next night. It was about 30 kilometers to get to the DMZ, and then they would take a tunnel that the CIA had that came out about one click south of the village. The movement would take them through Tondegon and Uijongbu. Most of it was rural. They would be going on foot since it was the best way to stay silent. Most every building along the route was rubble at this point anyway. The only thing to really worry about was zombies, of course. They had both seen them on previous movements, but they were slow and very decrepit.

During previous scouting missions they had seen a presence of activity, but never saw anything alive. They'd seen footprints, drag marks, and so on, but nothing actually moving in the area. Their most recent trip had been to make sure that the tunnel was still serviceable, and to verify that they could still make it across.

The problem with going across the DMZ on foot was that it was a minefield, and they didn't have the time or resources to try to clear a minefield that may have survived the apocalypse.

The next time for coms with Cheyenne was at 0900 local time, and they all needed to rest and eat. This is when nerves get on high, but the team had all experienced it before. Rahe was going to stay in the monitoring center, and the rest of them hit the rack for the night.

Sleep came and went for most of the team. Achilles dreamed about his daughter and family. She would be 6 or so right now. He didn't kid himself with the false pretense that she was alive, but his dad, who had been a Green Beret in Vietnam, was a survivor. If there was a way to keep the family alive, his dad would have been the one to make it happen. One thing that always made Achilles laugh was that his dad was always ready for anything, and when the shit hit the fan, he would have done what was needed to keep those in his charge alive. They had a beach house on Tybee Island, a little beach town outside of Savannah, Georgia. The home was on a little point, and if need be they could have gotten out via the 42 foot Grady White fishing boat his dad had at their dock. The old man had always told him that if they ever came for him ("they" meaning government spooks, vampires, aliens, zombies, and so on), he would make for a small island in the Bahamas that they all knew about. Achilles made a promise to himself, once this shit was all over with, he would take his team and search for all of their families. Soldiers or not, family is the most important after the mission is over.

Chapter 8

The DMZ

At 0900 hours they were all waiting when the call from Cheyenne came in. Cheyenne had already spoken with Captain Teeple, and was aware of the SAM site and the missile launch against the Osprey. They spoke about the mission, the new timeframe, and then Honcho, Eagle, and Achilles had a private conference.

The President himself led the discussion and that made Achilles a bit nervous. Since this all had gone down he had pretty much let Honcho do his thing with the team, so when the Commander in Chief himself stressed the importance of the issues at hand, Achilles sat up and listened intently.

"Colonel Mountjoy, this virus is nastier then we first thought. Our scientists here have been trying to figure out how we can get it back here, the sample from Patient Zero that is. We aren't sure that it will stay alive without a human host. We aren't sure if you have to bring the host back here, or if you can extract the virus. I want you to speak with Dr. Baker about this and do whatever is necessary in case we need a viable host to get this thing home. I just want you to know as the team leader that Dr. Baker is up to speed on what I am telling you, and you need to trust his gut feeling when the time comes."

Achilles said "Yes sir!" and saluted the President. The President returned the salute, and told Achilles to speak freely.

"Sir, I don't think that a member of the team is a viable solution if we have to provide a host. I think that we will have to play it by ear when it all goes down. Furthermore, if this isn't the correct facility, we will be back to square one. I don't want to get everyone's hopes up or down, we will just do our best and try to make this happen."

Honcho and Eagle both acknowledged this and told him to do his best for his nation, and the world. Honcho then updated Achilles, telling him that there were survivor groups in the United Kingdom, France and Spain, and many island countries that had little to no military. It wasn't even certain that they had been affected by the virus. "So if we are to get back on track and keep what our nation has worked to make for two hundred and fifty years, we need this mission to be a success." With that the communication died.

Achilles brought the team up to speed and had Stewy brief the team on what the plan would be if they found the facility. Stewy would try to extract the virus and contain it, then they would get the hell out of Dodge and make for the extraction site. Stewy knew the risks about containing it, and how he would try to handle it prior to coming on the mission. That's why he came, he had little to no faith in the other lab coats that he had been working with at Cheyenne.

With that, they started the backwards planning until they would move out. Gear would be checked, cross-loaded, and the route selected. Little details like order of movement were worked out, what to do if they encountered close or near contact, and plans for rally points or fall back points. They had five hours until they would start the movement. If everything went wrong, if they were separated, the plan was to come back to this bunker. There was enough food, power, and water to provide three years' worth of great living if someone didn't make it out to the extraction site. It was reassuring, but Achilles knew he wouldn't leave this place without every single member of his team.

They would move in a standard file formation, three to five meter separation, and they would form a loose circle with the shooters in the front in case there was contact. It was pretty standard for all of the team. The Browns and Big Joe would bring up the rear; Big Joe had even requisitioned an M-240G machine gun from the bunker. So the support by fire position would have a crew serve weapon and two sniper rifles. Big Joe was carrying so much weight that there was no question in anyone's mind to as how strong this man was.

Darkness fell and the team set out on their movement. They would make for the tunnel in the nine hours that they had before sunup. They would sleep in the tunnel, then assault the village the next night. Movement under the darkness was the safest, and that's what Achilles wanted. They started walking, or as most soldiers called it ruck marching for their target.

For the first three hours it was pretty much the same, move and move, and move. They took a break and a map check to make sure the road they had selected was the right one. Woody spoke up and told them that this was MSR One, and that he had flown over it many times while he was in the ROK (Republic of Korea). It was almost surreal, nothing moved, there was no wildlife, and every building looked like something out of a bad movie. This was what most of Japan looked like after World War II, but for the team, pictures had done it no justice.

Meat and Moon went ahead and were doing a small recon, They generally stayed about 500 meters in front of the rest of the team along with Rahe. They were scouting the route when they came upon something that none of them thought was real. There was a man sleeping, or who appeared to be asleep on the side of the road. Moon let Achilles know that they had contact and that they were checking it out. Two flashes from the red lens laser designator and the team knew where to link up.

Moon crept up to the man and nudged him with his weapon. That was all it took, the moan was the next thing they heard. It sat bolt upright; it was a zombie. Moon placed a shot right between its eyes and it went down. Stewy was on it like stink on shit, he got out a syringe and a pair of gloves, took a blood, skin, and brain sample and placed them into his kit. It was surreal how fast he made this happen. It made Achilles more certain than ever that they had selected the right lab rat to come on this mission.

They continued their route and moments turned to minutes and minutes turned to hours. They all seemed to be handling the march fine, maybe a blister here of there for Big Joe or possibly the Doc, but all in all they were in good shape. At around 0500 hours they were within a kilometer of the tunnel. Snyder spoke to Achilles about going ahead with a shooter to ensure it was still clear, and they all agreed it was for the best. Snyder and Rahe moved ahead and the group settled into a loose assembly area.

Within half an hour they returned and Ghost let the team know it was clear to go ahead and make for the tunnel. Not too shabby. They had made contact. Granted, they had only obtained samples, but at least it would help with research. They got to the tunnel and went inside. In Achilles' mind, this was probably the most amazing thing that they had come across. It was more than just a tunnel, it was a full blown concrete tunnel with three damn golf carts.

Ghost and Smoke got the carts prepped and told Achilles that they had been working on this tunnel, or rather the U.S. had been working on it for close to fifty years. It had been completed in early 2008, and since then American operatives had been using it to get important allies in and out of North Korea. Probably the most amazing thing was that it had power and working lights. Smoke let them know it would be about an hour's ride, and that there was a small area stocked with food and water before the other end.

The team split up into the three golf carts and started the drive to the other end. Who would have thought: golf carts and tunnels that led under the DMZ, a river, and a minefield. "What else did our nation do that no one would ever know about?" It really made Achilles think about things during the ride.

The team came to a halt towards the end of the tunnel. At the end was a large steel wall and a room. Smoke and Ghost led the team into the room and told them that this was the operations detachment headquarters. To be honest, it was way more than a room, it was a room that had a complement of beds and a communications center. By now it was close to 0600 hours, and they decided that sleep was what everyone needed more than anything.

It's a funny thing, but even in a tense situation most special operations and military members in general can sleep anytime, anywhere, and in any circumstances. This made Achilles chuckle to himself as within moments all of the team was sleeping tightly. Achilles took the time to write in his journal that was located on his pad device. He thought that this would help during the back brief if they ever made it back to Cheyenne Mountain and the remnants of the government. As he was writing sleep finally came.

At around 1500 hours the team started to rouse from sleep. As they were shaking off the cobwebs, Achilles got off the rack that he was sleeping on. Smoke had the screens up and operational and actually was working without smoking. He saw Achilles rise and told him that he was monitoring the area that had once been Propaganda Village. The amount of cameras that the CIA man was operating was quite frankly astonishing to Achilles, and from the vantage points that were being used he could see that there were actually footprints in and around what was once a city. This made him realize that they needed to rethink the plan a little and that the entire team would need to have a planning session before they went out to hunt under the cover of darkness.

In a short while, the entire Seeker element was up and around a table that was in the center of the room. Little Brown asked about making some coffee and that was when the difference between a special operations soldier and a regular Army soldier was made clear. It was actually Dr. Baker that brought it up before a member of the team.

"Josh, we can't drink coffee. The dead can actually smell us and anything that is out of the ordinary, so coffee would be a poor choice to try and get the blood flowing."

With that, Big Joe slapped the Doctor on the back and told him that was good thinking. Big Brown just smacked his son in the head and told him to quit acting like a damn cherry.

Smoke and Ghost laid out the situation for the rest of the team. They told them that the opening from the tunnel was actually a pile of false rocks and they would have to crawl out of it. There was a 50 foot clearing between the remains of the buildings and the opening, and they would have to move quickly and stay low while they were moving from cover to cover. The opening was on the side of a ridgeline, and there were actually a few blinds as hunters call them that the support by fire team could use; they wouldn't even have to leave the tunnel. This was handy for them, as they would be able to cover the team the entire time they were out and moving.

The plan was to wait until they were under the cover of darkness, and then the team would slip out and try to find the opening to the underground facility. They would have to wait a while to see if there was any movement, as this would aid them in finding a place to enter the facility. Smoke explained that they had not been up here since the reckoning, and their equipment at Stanley was unable to communicate with and/or operate the equipment here. As far as their earlier recons had gone, they had just been to make sure that they could get a team to this position.

The team took the opportunity to get into position and scout out their surroundings. The support team was taken to the firing position and fields of fire were laid out. Woody talked to the Browns about not exposing themselves, and Big Brown actually impressed him with his knowledge of sniper operations. They set radio frequencies to use and got their weapons ready for any action that could happen. Achilles thought to himself that they had been lucky so far. The fact that the zombie population had been decimated in this part of the world was due to the amount of high yield uranium loaded nuclear bombs that had torn this land apart.

Darkness was approaching and the team was ready to find out if there was anything amiss. Final coms were made for the day with the ship, and they knew that there wouldn't be any more contact with the ship once the satellite was gone from their area of operations. Ghost and Smoke had everything set and ready to go with the monitoring equipment and they all had their gear ready to move in a moment's notice.

Chapter 9

The City

Once it got dark, it got spooky and interesting at the same time. The team was monitoring the area, and the support by fire team was looking for anything moving. It was Meat that saw the first trace of movement on the monitor, and it was enough to send chills down the spines of every member of the team. For a city that was in shambles, one would think that there was no way that anything could have survived the devastation that the warheads had left in this area, but they saw that the Z's were in fact still there.

At first there was one. In less than half an hour there were close to fifty Z's that had come out of the same structure. Ghost pulled up the schematic of the underground facility that had come into the hands of the CIA prior to the apocalypse, and it fit the exact location that they had speculated housed the entrance to the facility.

Achilles came across the net and let the snipers know what to do: take out as many Z's with suppressed weapons as possible. The shooting began, and head-shots were being rained down upon the undead with lethal precision. Woody and Opie were even up with the Bravo Team and helping to take out as many as they could. It took the team close to half an hour of shooting to get most of the undead down, but at that point Achilles decided to get the team moving. He let the support element know the time frame.

"Alright team, we are going to enter through that opening. If we aren't back topside in six hours, that's your cue that something has gone wrong. Go back to Stanley and try to get an extraction. You can take that as a failure on our part. God willing we will be back and be on our way out of this hell-hole with you."

The team rallied on Achilles and they made their way across the barren wasteland. It was a short jaunt to the entrance of the facility, but any combat soldier carrying a load of gear and moving at full speed with a rush of adrenaline will tell you that it can seem like miles afterwards. The team entered the door and cleared the first room. That first room was no larger than an entrance to any government building. It looked like an unfinished apartment building with a dirt floor. There were no lights, and the only thing that made it any different from any other room that the group had come across in the past was the fact that there was a rather extravagant digital keypad at an enormous steel door.

This would be the first test that they would have to pass to get inside. "Security," was all that Achilles said. Moon got his pad out while the rest of the team set up in a half semi-circle guarding the door.

"Bravo Team, we are at the first door, not too sure how long our coms will hold out, anything out there?" said Achilles over the throat mic.

It was Big Joe that came back. "Negative, Boss." That was it, no long winded explanation, which what Achilles liked.

Moon was fast at work. He had the pad and tool kit out and was fast at work on the key pad. Achilles could see the sweat on his brow, but there was no complaining; he worked and ran the encryption software hacking protocols and within a few moments there was a click and they were in.

The door was 4 inches thick and it was made of solid steel. The team had no clue how the Z's were coming from the other side of it. When they cracked it open just a tad bit, they could see that inside it was illuminated and they would not need their night vision goggles any longer. They all knew that if there was security inside that this is when they would either hit it, set off an alarm, or be on the safe side of things.

Achilles put his hand on Moon's arm. "Moon, did the pad bring up any security protocols?"

"Yes, but they should have been disabled also. The only thing that we should have to worry about is guards."

As Achilles inched the door further open, he noticed that the map that they had was way wrong. This door opened into a hallway. It looked to be around 50 or so feet long, and there was a t-intersection at the end. The team all started moving toward the end of the hall, Achilles in the front, followed by Moon, Opie, Meat, Doc, and Woody bringing up the rear.

As they moved toward the t-intersection they couldn't help but notice how the only thing that was dirty were the footprints from the Z's that were now lying in a heap outside, and that they had only walked in the middle of the passageway. At the intersection the team could go left or right. On the left there was a door with a keypad, on the right there was a stairwell.

"Boss, all of the footprints go into the door, I think that we should avoid it," said Meat. Achilles agreed that at this point that was a good idea.

The team descended the stairs and came to a landing, where it started to get interesting. On the wall they found a schematic of the building. It would have been hard to figure out where to go or how to use it, since it was encoded in Korean, but with the pad device all they had to do was take a picture of it, use the encryption and hacking software that they had been given, and they had all the info that they needed right on the pad. It took a little while, but no one came up on them and they seemed to be in an area that nobody wandered through. They had been in the complex for under twenty minutes and they already had a map. The next step was finding a computer terminal where Moon and the Doc could try to get some vital information to get the team to the next step of the mission.

The map showed them that they would have to travel just under 300 meters and make five turns to get to the laboratory which they hoped contained the answers that they were looking for. They had a problem; they needed to go right past what looked to be the chow hall and the barracks. If they had deciphered the facility map correctly, there were no less than seven hundred and fifty of the Premier's finest soldiers and officers in this facility with him. This would create a huge problem for the team. Who knew how many of these soldier had been turned into brain eating, bone sucking Zombies at this point?

It was Opie who had the idea. "Sir, why don't we go get Big Joe, the Browns, and those two Spooks while we still can? We sure could use that firepower, besides, if we have to get out of here via their hangar by requisitioning an aircraft or something, they will need to be with us" That was a great point, and if they went any deeper inside the facility the other team would be cut off from them.

Meat and Woody went back for the Bravo Team, while Alpha Team got ready to move. They would do their best to avoid contact and make it to the lab. They hoped that at this hour they wouldn't have to fight with anyone and that most of these soldiers would be in their racks sleeping. As they waited they got that bit of edge that every soldier gets when they know an operation is starting to go in the direction of the unknown. The gaming types and generals call it the fog of war, but soldiers just dealt with it. The team all knew that this was just one of the things that they would have to deal with to make the ride home.

Meat and Woody came back with the Browns and Big Joe in tow. Woody explained how the spooks took the news. They had told him that they were "mission complete" at this point and would either meet them at the boat, or they would make their own way back to the home. This in a way pissed Achilles off, but on the other hand, it kept him from having to keep them safe. It was a win-win in his mind.

At this point they had yet to run into a patrol; they had been lucky, but they were bound to run into some sort of surveillance, whether it be thermal or cameras. Or they would trip some sort of door that had a sensor on it. Moon had been studying the layout that they had found for the better part of a half an hour. He knew which way they had to move, and had been talking it over with Achilles. They just needed to take a few moments to formulate the next part of the plan before they moved out.

Moon came up with a good and direct route as they reviewed the schematics. They would have to go by what they had narrowed down as the enlisted billeting "Housing" and the mess "Chow Hall" facilities. At this time of night there might be a few people going in and out, but hopefully they could get though there without being detected. First they would have to go down a few flights of stairs. The hard part would be the three security doors that appeared to have guarded stations that led to the labs. This was interesting to the team, because what they also saw on the map in this area was what appeared to the entrance to the Dictator's own private quarters. Even though the world was in shambles, they all knew that if the opportunity arose they would have to take the chance to take down a dictator in the name of freedom. Targets of opportunity do not always present themselves on a silver platter, and this time would be no different if the chance was given.

Achilles gave the order for the team to use suppressors and try to stay to knives and pistols with silencers. If they had to get into a firefight, they would be overwhelmed as soon as it got loud. The sheer numbers of bad guys and the possibility that they had any control over the undead population was just way too much of an unknown at this point. They would move in this order: Meat, Achilles, Moon, Big Joe, Doc, Big Brown, Little Brown, and Woody, with Opie bringing bring up the rear. It was his job to close doors and to make sure that there was no tail following them.

Chapter 10

The Mess Hall

As the team made their way down the corridor, they came to the mess hall. It was illuminated by red light and seemed to be nearly deserted. The best thing about this place was that every door had one of the electronic panels on it, which caused no problem for Moon. When they got to the door, they went in, fanned out to all sides and swept through it. The Browns stayed at the rear with Moon who worked on closing the security door, and the rest of the team went toward the rear to secure the rest of the large room.

Toward the back they found that there was more light; this was common in a mess facility with overnight workers getting food ready for the coming day's workforce hungry for breakfast. Opie and Meat went around the edges and took five workers by surprise, and in a few moment's time had them all corralled up and brought out to the center of the room. Big Joe and Woody made sure there were no stragglers about and that all of the freezers and offices were clear of enemy combatants.

Achilles' first question to the group was, "Who here speaks English? And who is in charge?"

They all looked nervous, and to be honest a few looked ready to shit themselves.

Who wouldn't be! They were living in a facility with zombies, they had a crazy dictator, and the outside world was a nuclear wasteland. And now a United States Special Forces Team was holding them point blank with automatic weapons. They had every right to be scared shitless.

It only took a minute or two, but the guy who looked to be in charge spoke up in pretty plain English. He said he was in charge and that he spoke some English; to be honest, he sounded as if he was from Brooklyn. At this point, Big Joe and Woody took the others to the back of the mess hall, flex cuffed them with zip ties and put them in a freezer. They were kind enough to pull the plug so that it wouldn't freeze them, and they even left the door cracked so that oxygen got inside.

Achilles started. "OK young man, here is the deal. My name is Col. Achilles and I am here on behalf of the United States Government. I am not here to kill you, and I really do not want to kill you, your friends, your officers, other soldiers, or your commander. I just need some information and then I need to get to the laboratory. Do you have any idea what the madman in charge of this place has done to the rest of the world?"

With that the cook just got a far off look in his eyes, one of those looks that Vietnam veterans get when they talk about losing friends back in the Nam. He almost broke down in tears before he even started talking. At that point the team was flabbergasted. They just looked at each other. Achilles looked at the cook and asked him if he needed a moment, but he said no, and that he would tell Achilles anything.

"I just need your word, Colonel, that you will not kill me, and if they catch you, make it look like you just subdued us." At a nod from Achilles, he started talking.

"My name is Jung Sung Wi, Head Cook, Freedom Facility. I grew up with my parents in New York City; I knew that we were from North Korea, Hell, I even knew that my dad was a spy. I was training to be a chef, but after 9/11 my dad had to get us home. Every single thing we did was monitored. We eventually got back in country, and my dad got his post back in the Ministry of Defense. I got promoted here as the head Chef. We use this facility as a place where the dignitaries hold briefings. It's kind of funny that the CIA thinks that it's just a fallout shelter, but most of the North Korean government is run right under their noses, or was run right under their noses, from *this* place. When the United Nations decided to nuke us, we were ready. The North has had the technology for years, and all of the missiles that we launched were just to keep them ignorant of our true potential in the arms race. The real secret, and probably the reason that you are here, is the Dark Matter. To tell you the truth, the Dictator knows that you will come. I am sure that he thinks there is no way that you will get in, that you will find it. He thinks those damn zombies from space will keep us safe! He has no damn clue. I went to NYU, I know that we have no clue as to what they are, how the Hell do things that are dead walk around? How do they have no heartbeat? How do they not die? This is all insane. Thank God there are only a few down in the lab." He hung his head and sniffled quietly when he was done.

Achilles and the team took a minute to digest the information while Big Joe roughed Jung up to put on a little bit of a show for the rest of his cooks. The team took the little time that they had and got ready to move. The next area of concern would be the first security door.

They were going to put Woody in a cook's uniform and have him go up to the door with a tray and cart to feed the sentries. This would get them all the way to the third door. This bit of information was huge, and Jung had given it to them freely.

The Doc stopped Achilles and told him that he needed a word. "Achilles, we have a problem."

"Yeah Doc, go ahead."

"I overheard Honcho and Eagle talking about something with the international space station and Dark Matter. They were sitting in our lab at Cheyenne and spit-balling about how the zombies were created. I know that I shouldn't know this, but they said that after the shuttle program was scrapped with the previous administration and all, the Chinese and the Russians had stumbled upon Dark Matter. Anyway, two cosmonauts were exposed to Dark Matter. If this is the same stuff from science fiction type books, you know, an energy source, maybe it altered their DNA sequence and this is what the North Koreans found? I know I am throwing a lot at you, but if this is it, when we hit this lab, we might all get exposed to something that may kill us all. You know the North Koreans might not have contained it correctly." The Doc paused for a moment, then continued. "The other thing I recall about that conversation was that the escape pod from the International Space Station landed, guess where? North Korea! We may be on a one-way mission. So what I am saying, Colonel, we may need to find the communications center also!"

Achilles nodded and spent a few moments mulling over this new information. Then after a quick brief from him, the team moved out. Woody led the way in his new outfit and the team stayed back, always keeping a corner between them. They made it past the barracks facility in this fashion. As they approached the first security door and guard station, Woody let them know that there was one guard and he was reading a book. The guard didn't even look up at Woody's approach, he just leaned down and hit a button to unlock the door. Woody pushed the cart though and propped the door open, put the tray on the security desk, and then slit the guard's throat. The guard died without a sound, unaware to the end that the facility had been breached.

They looked at the schedule and saw that they had four hours until the next change in shifts. This was the same schedule for the next two doors. Moon went to work on getting the door's electronics disabled, and they did a quick job of propping the guard up and making it look like he was reading his book in case anyone passed by.

They continued down the hall toward the second door and repeated the process. They had the same success, but almost got caught at the third door. This guard was a bit more alert; Woody almost missed with the knife, but quick thinking and having his off hand on a butter knife alleviated this issue.

After the third security door they were in the depths of the facility. They would need to access one more stairwell and then they would be on the lab level. They had to gain access through a door and then deal with a camera. Moon was quick at work and did a great job at hacking into the security protocols. It was pretty awesome to listen to him talk about how great the pad was, and how much he would have given to have one of them prior to all of this shit happening.

The team gathered together one last time as Achilles briefed them. He let them all know that this was where the proverbial shit could hit the fan. The mission was simple: they would split into three teams and then gather as much intelligence as they could. This level was the only place in the compound that had access to where they needed to go. Since there were now in essence three targets, they would need three teams.

Team One would be Woody and the Browns. They would go for the hangar. It was their job to get there, clear it, find a way to open the hangar door, and get a ride to the coast. Either an airborne asset, a submersible (which this place was rumored to have) or some sort of car, truck, tank, or whatever. They were to provide security when it came time for the team to exfil.

Team Two would be Meat and Big Joe. They would have the delightful task of getting to the Dictator and taking him down. If they couldn't get to him, they were to take out as many assets as possible and to rain as much terror upon the enemy as they could. That included blowing the hallway leading to this area, since the schematic had shown that this was the only way in and out of this area.

Team Three would be composed of Achilles, the Doc, Opie, and Moon. They would go for the lab. They would try to get the sample, research data, and whatever else they could find that the United States Government could use to help find a cure.

They took the last few minutes to make sure that all the radios were working and synced, all gear was cross checked, weapons were checked and rounds and explosives were set. They went back to the last security check point and rigged it with explosives. According to the security checklist they had about an hour or so before people would begin their morning routines.

Achilles made a mental note. That gave the team a little over twenty-four hours before they would be late for pickup by the Chung Hoon. Captain Teeple seemed like a reasonable Skipper, but in these uncertain times, would he wait for these men? It seemed like he would, but who knew these days.

Chapter 11

Team One

Hollywood and the Browns made their way toward the hangar. It was a long corridor, and according to the schematic they should not come across any security. Just as Woody thought to himself that they shouldn't have any trouble, Big Brown brought up the fact that the "Commie bastards" were probably pretty damn complacent now anyway. There weren't anything but zombies left to give them any problems, so if the hangar doors were shut, they shouldn't have to worry about much of anything.

As they made the turn to the last hallway that would lead them to the hangar they heard voices. Woody held up a fist that signaled a freeze: common military sign to not make a sound, step or even take a breath. He inched along the hall and pulled out ever so slightly a telescoping dental mirror. He used this device to peer around the corner.

What he saw nearly made his heart and mind stop in horror. There was a North Korean officer dressed in his uniform, and he was talking to two sentries. They were freaking zombies, and they were standing at attention! They weren't standing at perfect attention, but they damn sure were trying to. The strangest thing was that they were moving their heads up and down, and they seemed to understand what the officer was telling them to do!

The officer then left and went on his way to a part of the hangar that Woody couldn't see. the two sentries went back on patrol, one to the left, and one to the right. Woody looked at Little Brown and said, "Take this mirror and watch this corner, if someone starts to come this way, let me know. I have to talk to Achilles!"

"Six, this is Three, over."

"Go for Six."

"Six, we have an issue. I just witnessed firsthand an officer give two Z's orders, and they did not eat him. They nodded their heads and understood what he said, then went about their merry way, do you copy?"

"Three, uh… roger… ."

"Two, this is Six, did you copy what Three just said, over?"

"Six, this is Two, I got a good read. Did I hear that right, the deaders can take orders and don't eat the Northerners?"

"That is affirmative, make sure head shots count …. break, we do not know numbers, everyone proceed with caution. Six out!"

Woody looked at the Browns and asked them if they understood what that meant; they both looked a little shaken. He addressed Big Brown directly. "Big man, whatever you do, do not pull out that Python," referring to the .44 Magnum with the 8 inch barrel that he had refused to let go of, "unless the bad guys open up and things get loud, got me?"

Big Brown gave him a thumbs up.

After a little bit of time passed, they didn't see the sentries or anyone else come back into sight. They looked high and low, but from their vantage point they really couldn't see that much. Woody made the command decision to move down the hall toward the entrance to the hangar. It was a 20 foot walk that opened into an impressively sized aircraft hangar. It reminded Woody of the place where this entire project that he was on had started. It was huge, and that was probably why they could not see any of the sentries or the officer that was in charge of them.

There was a lit up office to the left. It was a hundred and fifty meters away, and the good old North Koreans even had fire lanes. "Safety first," was all that Hollywood thought. They crept along the wall, and kept a look out for the sentries. Ten feet from the office they could hear music, and within five feet they could smell a cigarette burning. No, this wasn't the United States, it was a Communist country.

The officer was sitting in the office facing a computer and working when Hollywood put the bullet through his temple. All that was heard was the slide clicking from the H&K USP.45 Semi-automatic; the quickness with which he kept the officer from hitting the ground and making noise was impressive.

The office was very useful. Big Brown and Woody made use of it; they found keys to aircraft and logbooks, and decided that they would have the best luck with a submersible vehicle, or a submarine. There was one that would fit the entire team, and since there was a

SEAL on the team, hopefully he could drive the damn thing. Woody's first choice would have been a Russian era helicopter, but who know what kind of air defense system that the North Koreans still had operational. According to the schematic, the underwater system launched this sub straight out into the Pacific.

As they were getting the keys and codes for the sub, Little Brown said something no one wanted to hear: "Dad, we have company!"

Chapter 12

Team Three

Achilles and his team went left down the three corridors that they could choose from. He stopped when they were out of earshot from the other two teams and told the other two shooters that he needed a minute to brief them on the situation a bit further.

"Guys, there is a little more to our situation. The Doc thinks that something deeper is going on. This wouldn't be the first time in our days as Operators that we have gone into something blind, but this may be way bigger than anything we've done before. I am telling you this because we may have to think fast, and

Moon, you may have to get us online with Cheyenne quickly, and I mean quickly. Do either of you know anything about Dark Matter?"

Moon chuckled a little. "Yeah, Boss, it is supposed to be 4th dimension type stuff that they were messing with in Switzerland. They wanted to use it as an energy source."

"Well, Moon, the Doc says that during our little time travel journey, the prior administration scrapped NASA, and the Communist countries may have gotten to work on the International Space Station. Then they did something up there, and all the cosmonauts and Chinese astronauts had to use the escape pods to jettison home. Funny thing, the pod landed in North Korea. Guess where the CIA says that pod is located? Right damn here! And then to put the icing on the cake, The UN Security Council tells the world that the North Koreans have the bird flu by trying to create super soldiers, and instead they have created zombies. The UN nukes North Korea, North Korea counter launches, and we have the zombie-fucking apocalypse."

The whole team including the Doc just stared at Achilles with open mouthed stares. The Doc started with, "I guess you put that together with what Hollywood told you?"

"Yes Doc, it all makes sense. The problem is, I don't think that Honcho or Eagle know what we are really dealing with. Maybe they have a hunch or something, but when those two CIA nut-jobs ran out on us, that was way too convenient."

"Achilles," said the Doc. "I have this serum, I really don't know what they planned on me using it for, in case we get bit, I don't know, but the bottom line is I really have no clue as to what we are going to get from here. If we get a sample we are going to get exposed. If we get back on that ship, the exposure would contaminate and expose that entire crew of that ship. Once we are exposed, I am going to have to demand that we all take this shot. I have enough for the entire team, hell, if I find something that the Koreans have, we better take that also, agreed?" Achilles nodded his head up and down.

The team moved down the hall and came to a security door. Moon pulled out his pad and began to hack it to get it open. This was the first one so it would take a while. The rest of the team took up security positions.

Chapter 13

Team Two

Meat and Big Joe went down the long hallway that led to the Dictator's Quarters. They knew from the radio transmission that there were bound to be Zombie guards, human guards, and possibly some sort of slaves that this sick man would have. He had been known over the years to have repressed his citizens, but what dictator over time had not done the same.

As they came to the end of the hall there were only three doors, and all three of them were open. They looked at each other. One left, one right, one in the center. The one on the left was dark, the one in the center was trimmed in gold (what had to be the quarters of the supreme ruler), and the one on the right smelled like a brothel. That was probably were his harem was. Big Joe smiled at Meat and made a nasty jest. Meat smiled and mouthed, "Maybe later." There was little illumination in the room, and they went in with night vision on. Meat went left and Big Joe went right.

The room was big, but not too big, kind of like the size of a house in the States, just like a ground floor with no walls. In the middle of the room against the back wall was a bed, and in it was the Dictator with two naked women sprawled about the bed with him. The most disconcerting part to the team was that there were eight zombie guards along the back wall all just standing there; they looked to be in a comatose state. To the right of the bed was a hallway that was not on the schematic. If the shooting started, they would have to deal with guards possibly coming from the other room behind them to the left, the dictator leaving through the unmarked door, eight zombie guards, who knows how many harem women; it was getting complicated. They slipped back out of the room and back down the hallway. They would need to talk to Achilles before going any further with their part of the mission.

"Six, this is Two, we may have some complications. We have three doors and have located the target. Target has eight Z's guarding him. There is a door in his room that is not on the schematic on your side of the facility. There's a guard quarters that we have yet to check, there is possibly a harem, our suggestion is to neutralize the guard quarters, harem, take the leaders down then the Z guards……How copy?"

"Good copy, Two, Break… Break…"

"Six, this is One, we have inbound Z's in the hangar, we are going guns on silent, may get hairy, might have to blow door three… are we sure that no one can get past that door?"

Moon looked up at Achilles. "Pretty sure, boss, if that schematic we downloaded is right…"

"Break, One, do what you need to do. Two, silent as possible, I would put down the leader, pop smoke and head our way rickety split, more guns to stop the guards. We can blow door three, Hell, we might have to blow the lab door. Good copy all?"

Two clicks came back.

Meat stepped back into the room, took about ten silent steps forward, put the red dot of his laser designator right over the heart of the North Korean dictator and pulled the trigger. The only sound was the slide of the pistol, but it was enough to stir the zombie guards. They looked around at one another. Meat thought for a moment that they knew he was there, but then the one closest to the bed smelled the air, looked to its left then dove on the bed and started to devour the Dictator. All of the rest of the zombies rapidly followed suit and leaped on the bed; he had started a feeding frenzy. The women woke up and started screaming in horror as they quickly became covered in gore and then were ripped to shreds by the Z's. Meat turned on his heel and he and Big Joe ran like there was no tomorrow. Joe popped a CS grenade into the Harem and another into the guard quarters as Meat planted a remote detonator on all three doors.

"Six, this is Two, Target eliminated. Blood caused the Z's to wake up, they ate his ass. Detonators placed, we need to go loud and I mean now, this place is going to wake up, and I mean fast!"

With that, Achilles clicked the detonator placed at door three and the roof caved in; the only way the team was getting out now was through the hangar or another route.

Big Joe and Meat ran as fast as they could toward the lab. By now every single alarm in the facility should be going off, but to their surprise there was no loud alarm. No bullhorn, no alarm, no flashing lights, no fire alarm, no sprinkler, no nothing.

Chapter 14

Team One and Three - The Lab

As soon as the charges went off the door slid open. Achilles and Opie had their weapons up and at the ready. Moon was storing his pad was making his way toward them as Meat and Big Joe rounded the corner. At the same time he could hear Woody telling the Browns over the radio to "take them out and to fall back into the office." Things didn't sound good in the hangar, and he would let Woody do his thing without bugging him.

The security door opened into what is generally called a clean room, or a room where one would go from the outside to a sterilized area. There was another door leading to a room in which a person would go through a system that blew cleansers at them to clean them off. There was a red light in the corner.

The Doc spoke up. "That light generally shows that there is a breach in the lab, all we have to do to get through the next door is push that green button and that door will open. We will get hit by a bunch of air, but that should be it."

Achilles looked at the team, then said that he would go first just to check.

Opie held a hand up. "Boss, let me do it, we don't know what is on the other side. It could be booby trapped, I'll go!"

Big Joe muscled his way up, said two guns were better than one, and at a nod from Achilles they pushed the button, then entered and the door whooshed shut. Fifteen seconds later they exited and the rest of the team could see the muzzle flashes through the two sets of doors. Then Opie came across the net: Clear.

The rest of the team went through. It was a strange sensation, and on the other side the Doc told the team that he really didn't think it was in operating order. There were two dead North Korean guards on the other side. They had been ready when Big Joe and Opie came out, and Joe actually took a round to the chest; thank God for ballistic armor or, in other words, a bulletproof vest. He would be sore, but he was a big guy.

There were a few computer terminals and Moon went to work doing his thing. The Doc was busy gathering anything he could. The rest of the team was looking around and it led them to one final door. It was a door that looked like something out of a movie, more a vault than a door; it was sealed from their side, with a giant rotating handle. They couldn't make out what was on the other side, but they could see movement. There were windows but they were fogged over.

The bottom line was that it was go time, it was now or never. The rubble that separated the team from the North Koreans wouldn't take forever to clear, and from the sound of things on the radio Woody and the Browns had their hands full. Achilles decided to take the time to check in on them, since they were essentially going into a vault and he had no clue as to whether their communications gear would work inside.

"Three, this is Six, sitrep…"

"Six, this is Three. We are engaging multiple Z's and they are fucking shooting back at us… they can't aim worth a shit, but they seem to be able to coordinate with each other, so we are pinned down in an office. We have the keys and codes to a Sub, it's the best option, but we might need some help getting our asses out of here, over…"

"Roger Three, we are going into what we think is the lab, we are inbound as ASAP, keep your heads down, the cavalry is coming when we can, out."

The entire team knew what was going on, and the shooting was apparent in the background. They knew that the team in the hangar would not be able to hold out forever, so they had to move fast. Whatever was inside that vault was going to bare its ugly teeth as soon as they opened the door.

Meat started to spin the handle and the rest of the team had their weapons at the ready. It seemed to take an eternity but the handle stopped spinning and the door started to swing open. The team stepped in and they were amazed. The room was bathed in white. There were four scientists inside and they were all in lab coats. They all looked up and seemed as shocked as the soldiers that were looking at them. On the far wall there was another room that was separated from the laboratory; the entire wall was glass, and the team couldn't tell what was on the other side.

Meat, Big Joe, and Achilles all spread out and moved quickly to secure hostages. Moon kept his weapon leveled at the only scientist that didn't get up from his chair. He didn't even seem to be bothered. They all stated to speak in Chinese to one another, and the one seated said in plain English, "I knew this day would come." Before the soldiers could cross the room the three that could stand had fallen to the ground. They started to foam at that mouth, and the scientist that was seated started to laugh maniacally. He told the soldiers to lower their weapons or they would all be exposed.

At that point, they all just looked at one another. The doctor or scientist or whatever he was sat back in his chair and looked up at them. He asked who was in charge. Achilles stepped forward and said he was, and identified himself as Colonel Achilles, United States Army. This got a rather long-winded laugh, and then a sigh.

"OK, Colonel, since I know that there is no longer a United States or any other country, you can play that game. I am Doctor Honji Woo. That was my research team, and they were hooked to their seats. They knew that they couldn't stand up or they would be injected with cyanide. It is part of the job that our supreme ruler seemed to think necessary. I rather thought it was foolish, but those fools forgot that rule. So here we are, and they are dead. Now, if someone would be so kind as to unhook the syringe in my back, I will not be injected. If I get injected, well then, the dead man's protocol goes into effect and this room gets the exposure treatment."

Achilles nodded to the Doc and he walked up to the scientist and helped him get the syringe out. At that point the scientist got to his feet, thanked him and started to stretch. For a small man he was quick to try to grab Dr. Baker in a chokehold. Moon put him down with a single shot directly to the forehead. Then the team went to work, Moon got to work on the computers and the Doc looked for anything of value on the desks.

It was Big Joe that told Achilles that he better get over to the window and "take a look at this... ."

Chapter 15

Team Two - The Hangar

The three members of Team Two were inside the office and were attempting to return fire as they could not really see where it was coming from. It had been over ten minutes since they had heard from Achilles, and Hollywood knew that the Zombies would be coming for them. They would have to fight their way out. The major problem they faced was that there was no way to know how many Z's were on the outside waiting for them.

"Big Brown, hit that light switch." Woody was so mad at himself for not doing it in the first place, but shit happened fast on an op, and he wasn't perfect. They all were scanning through the doorway and trying to identify the targets; with the light out, they knew that in a moment or two they would start to get their night vision back.

After the light went out, shooting from the zombies actually stopped. The hangar itself was bathed in red light, it was dull enough that it enabled them to put on their goggles and that would be good enough to give them the advantage that they needed. They had the keys and codes that they needed to get the sub running, and hopefully they would be able to get the damn thing out into open water and link up with the ship.

"OK fellas, we need to get out of this office, find that boat and secure it." Big Brown took the lead, as far as he could tell there looked to be three to four zombies outside, and they looked confused as all get out once the lights had gone off in the office. The team moved as one, they swept out of the office and started shooting. Big Brown got his first target with a great shot to the forehead, Little Brown hit one with a three round burst then combat rolled to his left and found cover behind a stack of tires, and Woody hit one in the temple with a quick shot. They all were safely behind cover, and continued to scan the area.

"Anyone have eyes on the fourth target?" was all that Hollywood said. He got a negative from both of the Browns. He heard shuffling from his right, turned almost in time but not soon enough, and watched in horror as Little Brown had his head ripped from his torso. The sheer strength that the Zombie used was amazing to watch, and the fact that he hadn't even heard it was downright scary.

Big Brown was on the Zombie in a flash. Hollywood watched as Big Brown shot the Zombie in the back of the head and put it down. Then the elder sank to his knees in front of his son's body and his tears came pouring down. Hollywood had no words to console the man who at this point had lost what was left of his family. Sure, Little Brown had known the risks; he had been a soldier and survived a tour in Iraq. He had come willingly, had made through this horrible wasteland, only to die by a fucking zombie that was created by a madman.

Big Brown wept for a few moments, touched his son's torso, said a few silent words, then started to pick his body clean of ammunition and other things that they could use. He looked up at Hollywood and nodded. All he said was, "If one of them bites me, send me to my family." There was a silent communication between the two at that moment, a nod and an unspoken agreement between soldiers that would last a lifetime.

They spent the next few minutes clearing the remainder of the hangar. There were no more zombies in the area. They found the submarine, started the checklist and got it operational. Hollywood and Big Brown were amazed that the pad had the damn Technical Manual on it, what would Uncle Sam think of next? Well, if he ever came back to life.

"Woody, this is Achilles, do you copy, over?"

"Go for Woody…."

"Roger, we are securing vital information at this time, we are thirty mikes from exfil, sitrep," Achilles requested.

"Roger, sub is secure. We have a KIA at this time. Little B is down for the count. Sub is the exfil and checklist is initiated."

"Roger, we are securing cargo at this time, we will be en route to your local ASAP, out." Achilles looked somberly at the rest of his team; they took a moment to reflect on their fallen comrade in silence, then they got back to work.

Back at the sub, Hollywood got to work on the checklist while Big Brown provided security at the hatch that led to the inside of the vehicle. According to the readout inside the submarine, they would have a straight shot down this path to the Sea of China, where they could rendezvous with the ship and be on their way back to the States.

Chapter 16

Spacemen

"Jesus, Mary, and Joseph!" was all that came out of Opie's mouth, followed by a his vigorous signing of the cross. The Doc was still working with Moon to get as much data from the scientists' workstations and hard drives as possible, but what the team had discovered was a game changer. The window that Big Joe led Achilles to showed them what the scientists had been studying. And this was exactly what the Doc had spoken to Achilles about.

There was a room roughly about 300 feet by 300 feet, and 50 feet high. Inside there was a spaceship, or more precisely the International Space Station Emergency Escape Pod, and four Astronauts, Cosmonauts, or whatever strapped to tables in their zombified states. "Doc," said Achilles, "you'd better get over here and take a look at this!"

The team was stupefied by this new development. Achilles and the Doc had already known what was probably going on, and that was only because the Doc had shared the theory less than an hour earlier with Achilles. The rest of the team stared through the window with open mouths and looked at Achilles with the "What now look?"

"Woody, can you get the radio up and running on the sub? If so, I need a secure link to the boat, or to Cheyenne ASAP."

"Roger… Stand-by… ."

While Hollywood was working on the radio, Achilles made the command decision to split the team. "Moon, you go with Big Joe and head to the hangar, try to get that radio up and running and get me a secure link to the boat or Cheyenne. I need some answers before we crack this next door open."

Before they even left the lab, the Doc told them to wait. He chuckled, then told them that he would have Honcho on line in a moment. He couldn't believe it but they freaking had Internet here, just like at Cheyenne. Thirty seconds later, Achilles was staring at some major at Cheyenne Mountain asking for his identifier.

After giving his string of code words and identifiers, and waiting for another ten minutes, Honcho was looking right back at him. Achilles briefed him about what had happened so far, and then brought the SECDEF "Secretary of Defense" up to speed on what they were looking at, and also how they were planning to exfil. That way Honcho could contact Captain Teeple and let him know about the rendezvous.

"Holy shit, they really did find the Escape craft. We only speculated that was why the Chinese were so eager to get onboard and press everyone into the release of nuclear weapons. Colonel, when this all went down, it was a bad time. The video footage was so bad, intel was terrible, and we had no Americans on the space station at that point. We knew they had or thought they had created zombies, and all of the UN Security Council decided that nuclear attacks had to be done."

"Well sir, there are four damn astronauts strapped to tables in a room, we have all of the data from the hard drives that they have been studying, we have put down the secondary target, and their version of Z's can actually fire weapons and seem to be semi-cognizant. We have one KIA at this point, and have a ride to the ship, what are your orders at this time?"

"At this time I would suggest that you get a sample from one of the Z's, but do not risk any further exposure."

Right after Honcho said "exposure" the timing couldn't have been any more significant. A red light started flashing and on the computer screen where the lead scientist had been sitting a message flashed. "INPUT SECURITY CODE FOXTROT, YOU HAVE THIRTY SECONDS BEFORE SECURITY PROTOCOLS ARE INITIATED."

"Achilles, what that fuck was that?" Honcho asked. The team looked at one another in apprehension; the Doc and Moon were frantically scanning the information on their pads that they had taken from the facility's computers before they scrubbed them clean of information.

"Sir, I have no clue!"

A recorded voice began to count down: "10, 9, 8, 7, 6, 5, 4, 3, 2, 1."

From the ventilation came a hissing noise, and the door to the room they were in closed; at the same time the door to the laboratory with the astronauts opened, and the team was now exposed to whatever was inside the facility. The adjoining door that led to the laboratory that was the size of a small warehouse opened up, and the team just all stood there aghast.

Honcho started barking orders. "Achilles, keep this line open, we need video, and samples of everything in that room. We will coordinate from our end with Captain Teeple, you guys will have to ride home isolated. Dr. Baker, I don't know how good that serum is that you have on you, but I suggest that you better get to work on injecting yourselves with it."

"Roger that sir, we will keep this line open. We have to get moving, I am not sure how long we can keep the bad guys on the other end of our fallen tunnel, and more than that, we need to get the hell out of here; we will be outgunned at least thirty to one."

"Roger that Achilles, keep someone monitoring this uplink so they can keep us informed, we are getting our people here working on it."

"Ok, let's get what we came for," was all that Achilles said to the team. They entered the lab and knew that they were way out of their league, element, or even their time. The room looked like something out of a movie. There were four astronauts strapped to tables, and they were all snapping their teeth as the team went inside. Stewy was looking for anything on the PAD that had pertinent information in the data that they had extracted.

Achilles quickly began issuing directives. "Opie, we need a sample from one of those things, have Meat help you get blood, urine, mucus, and whatever else the Doctor needs. Moon, help the Doc with what he is looking for. Joe, keep Cheyenne updated with what we are doing down here, and for the love of God, everyone look for anything vital that we need to take with us."

At this point Achilles knew that reality was setting in for the entire team. They had fought across the country, crossed the Pacific, made their way through a secure North Korean compound, and now they had all been exposed to the virus. "Doc, how much time do you think we have before it takes effect?"

"I have no clue sir, shit, I don't even know if it's airborne, but the plain and simple fact is we are all probably fucked!"

At that moment, while Meat and Opie were gathering samples, Meat muttered "FUBAR" under his breath, and they all looked at each other and repeated it. FUBAR, or Fucked Up Beyond All Recognition is an old slang term that military men have used forever. It's one of those words that you say when saying "Fuck it" just doesn't cut the mustard.

"Achilles, this is Woody."

"Go, over…"

"Roger, we have Little Brown's remains on the sub, we are ready to get out of here, and I don't think that we have a whole lot of time. Big Brown says he can hear them trying to cut through the debris."

"All right guys, five mikes and we are out of here, Opie are you good to go?"

With that Opie nodded his head as he was putting the last of the samples in the secure case. The Doc pointed out that a skin sample might help, and Opie said "Fuck a skin sample!" then cut off the former astronaut's right hand and put it in a bag and placed it in the case. No one said a word.

Moon spoke up. "Hey guys, I got something here." The Doc was peering over his shoulder at his PAD and saw it also. "Guys, look for a safe somewhere on the north wall," and with that they found what indeed looked like a safe. Moon quickly managed to get the safe open and stepped back.

Inside Achilles pulled out a canister that had a green looking fluid in it, and notes that had been sitting right beneath it.

The team got ready to move, and Achilles took a minute to talk to Honcho. "We will be coming out at this lat and long, make sure that the boat and the Skipper are prepped for us. Also, we need a secure place to be separated from the crew, and Dr. Baker will need scientific equipment to determine if what we have found is any help. One more thing sir, if we are Zombies when we come out, tell the Skipper and the crew that there's a case that will be in one of the packs, it will have all of our data, and the serum. Achilles out."

Chapter 17

The Sub and Back to Sea

The team got on the submarine and secured the hatch. The first thing they realized was that Woody and Big Brown were right there and didn't even try to quarantine themselves from the rest of the team. All that they said was "Where we go one, we go all." The team all noticed the remains of Little Brown, wrapped carefully in a blanket on the floor. They bowed their heads for a moment, then moved quickly about their business.

Meat and Woody got the sub moving. According to the automated controls they would be underground in the tunnel for the next ten hours, and then they would be on the eastern side of Korea in the Sea of Japan. The sub was pretty easy to control. Since Meat had been a SEAL in a former life, he had a working knowledge of U.S. submarines, and the automated controls synced up with the PAD controls with a few adjustments.

Big Joe and Opie went ahead and cleared the rest of the sub just in case. They found some usable supplies as far as food and water were concerned. The team took a few minutes to get settled and then Achilles asked if they should try to close the tunnel behind them. Meat and Woody looked at each other, and said why the hell not. They then prepped and fired the aft facing torpedo tubes and hoped for the best. They would never know that they had indeed sealed the fate of the compound, as the torpedoes did their job and the entire compound collapsed.

The team gathered and it was clear that Moon, Stewy and Achilles had been talking about the situation. They all knew that they had been exposed; they were all feeling the telltale signs of the virus. Stewy looked at the team and told them they had two choices:

"Here is the deal. We can take the shots that I have; they have been tested and no one has recovered from the virus, all I know is that it slowed it down, and to be honest, that sounds to me like a slower death. On the other hand, if these notes we took are correct, they may have been the pieces of the research that we were missing at Cheyenne. I think that we should take the shots, and then work on combining their information with what I have and hope for the best once we get on the ship."

The team looked around, it was the best information that any of them had, and they knew that if they were going to live, well then they had to do something and do it quickly. After a little bit of debate, Achilles and the team all took the shots, and they all bitched and moaned that they hurt like hell. Big Brown even passed out, and this got everyone in better spirits. They would be in the sub for another hour or two at least, and they went to work trying to figure out what to do with the notes and serum that they got from the laboratory.

Between Opie, Moon, and Stewy, they went to work on the PAD. They also used the computer on the sub and in a little bit of time had made a lot of headway. They would need some of the medical equipment from the ship to spin the serum, but they knew that it was the only shot they had if they wanted to live.

The rest of the ride was pretty somber. They took time to reflect about Little Brown, Achilles said a few words, and Big Brown talked about how proud he was of the man that his only remaining son had become. They wrapped his body in a tarp, and would bury him at sea when they surfaced.

Meat was manning the communications system when he got the first contact with the Chung Hoon. It was waiting for the sub at the predetermined point. Captain Teeple explained that they would be using the Helicopter Hangar as their secure location, and they would pull alongside the sub. They would climb up, go inside, and they would then be put on lockdown until they were let off of the ship in the Puget Sound. The Skipper assured the team that they had all of the supplies, beds, food, water, and medical equipment that they would need to try to, in his words, "save their asses."

The sub surfaced next to the ship, Meat set it to scuttle itself in half an hour, and the team said a silent goodbye to Little Brown as they put him overboard. They loaded their gear and climbed up the netting that had been hung down the side for easy access to the Helicopter Hangar so that they could be put on lockdown while they crossed the Pacific Ocean. They went inside their new home, and found a note from the Skipper.

"Colonel Mountjoy, I hate to have to lock you guys down, but I have to do this for the safety of the crew. You will have time to speak with Honcho daily at the com station that we have set up. Anything that you need from me, contact me via the phone on the wall. We are all hoping for the best, be safe and we hope that this works."

The team settled in and got to work. Moon, Opie, and Stewy were working on the serum, and everyone else did whatever they needed to help them out. They would be at sea for at least nine days, and they hoped that at the end they would still be human… and alive. The first night came and they all settled in and tried to get some rack time. Achilles looked around at his team before nodding off. He noticed that Moon spent a little while praying prior to going to sleep. He thought about this and wondered why the hell not, at least his men all showed some sort of hope. Big Brown was in a bit of a mindless state, he had lost the last remaining member of his family, and Achilles knew that at some point all those emotions were going to come out and when they did, things might get ugly. Big Joe was telling jokes and some story about wrestling with some other superstar.

At some point in the night Meat woke Achilles up and told him that Honcho was on the horn and needed to talk to him. Achilles got up and walked over to the video monitor and put on the headset.

"God Damn son, you look like shit! Have you guys even taken the time to clean up?" That got Achilles to smile, and he straightened himself up in his chair. "Sir, we were all working on these notes and helping Dr. Baker. I am sure we will all get cleaned up in the morning."

"Good to hear, son. My scientists here have been going over what Moon and the Doc sent them last night, and to be honest it is a long shot, we don't have any clue what it will do to you, but they think that his calculations are correct. We want you guys to take the shots that Dr. Lyons will have finished in the morning. After you guys clean up, mind you, and then Dr. Lyons will come in a hazardous material suit and strap you all down. He will then administer the shots and monitor you. If it works, we think that you will at least not turn, and not be contagious. He will then test you, and if he gives the all clear, well then it is up to Captain Teeple on what to do with you guys."

"Roger that sir. If it doesn't work, we have the case, and it has everything that you guys need in it."

"God Speed, son," and with that, Honcho ended the uplink.

The team got up, and Achilles got everyone to clean up, shave, and get prepped. They had a small meal and he went over the plan. No one seemed to think it was crazy, and Doc Baker actually was very reassuring to the entire team.

"Guys, the people that are at Cheyenne are the best from the CDC, they got them out as soon as it happened, and they have been working nonstop on this. The data that we provided to them was the missing piece; I think that we can hope for the best here."

The serum was ready and the needles were prepped. The team strapped each other down and Opie was the last one. He remained unstrapped. This was done purposely so that he could at least say goodbye to his brother in case the worst happened. Dr. Lyons came in, gave his brother a hug through his giant hazmat suit, and then strapped him down.

He gave the shots to the team one at a time. Achilles went first, and as soon as it hit him, it was like fire had been injected into his arm and was spreading throughout his body. He screamed and thrashed but the restraints kept him down. It took Doc Lyons a few minutes to administer the shots to everyone and by then they all were going through the same effects. Doc Lyons had the video rolling and within five minutes the team was all asleep. An hour later he walked around and took vitals on all of the patients. They had very low heart rates, their breathing was slow, and they all showed signs of being in a low-grade comatose state.

Three hours into his rounds he got the video uplink and sent the data to the doctors, scientists and Cheyenne. They all seemed just as baffled as he; the team seemed to be fine, but there was no reason for the comatose state that they were in. The specialists conferred, then Doc Lyons hooked the team up to monitors and left the room so that he could continue with his other work. He would continue to check on the team periodically and report to Cheyenne on any progress.

Five days had passed when Doc Lyons noticed the first change in the patients. They all seemed to be a little bit bigger, as their muscle tone was increased, and to the trained eye they seemed to be growing physically. He took blood, urine, and mucus samples and looked over the data. They all seemed to have zero trace of the virus in their body, but on the molecular level the changes were phenomenal. They had more red and white blood cells, and they were physically perfect in every test that he ran. He noticed while checking their pupils that every member of the team now had dark black eyes; he saw that all of their hair had fallen off of their heads. He reported this back to Cheyenne and also uploaded the data that he was getting from the samples.

On day seven he was woken up by Captain Teeple. Doc Lyons and the Skipper watched a monitor as the team started to wake up, one by one, in the same order that they had been given the shots. Doc Lyons looked at the Skipper and told him that they had no trace of the virus, so he felt safe going in to unstrap them and run some preliminary tests. The Skipper told him to be careful, and Doc Lyons nodded, then entered the hangar without any sort of hazardous material suit on.

He stopped above Achilles and asked him "How are you feeling?"

Achilles looked at him and said, "I feel great Doc, a little parched, and a little sore where you put that shot in me, but I feel great. How long was I out?"

"Seven days, you guys have all been out seven days. We are going to unstrap you all, but you need to stay on your bunks so that we can run a few tests. Does anyone feel weird, faint, dizzy, anything out of the ordinary?"

Moon spoke up. "Doc, can you tell that guy that is typing to stop hammering on those keys, it is killing my ears!" The rest of the team acknowledged the same thing.

"Guys, no one is in here typing, are you sure that is what you hear? I don't hear anything."

Opie spoke up. "Dickie, I hear it too, find out where it is coming from for God's sakes!"

The Skipper was at the door. He said the typing was not anywhere near the team, but was in fact in an adjoining room that they had set up to monitor the team. "Gentlemen, are you all telling me that you can hear that?" They all looked up and said that they indeed could.

The next two days flew by in a flash. Stewy and Doc Lyons tested everything they could with the team. They already had learned that they had increased metabolism, increased hearing, eyesight, strength, and reflexes. They ate more like a bear would eat, a regular MRE has around 5,000 calories in it, and they were each eating six or seven of these per day. They all seemed like a better or more finely tuned version of their former selves.

They briefed Honcho on what was going on and what they were finding out about one another.

"Sir, we are all bigger, stronger, and faster than we were previously. It seems we can hear and see way better, we have larger appetites, and do not seem to tire very easily. We have no traces of the virus. The main problem is that we used up every bit of the serum that we took from North Korea to make the shots. We have the data and the specimens, but who knows what we can recreate and how quickly…"

Honcho had a huge smile on his face. "I am just glad you guys are good to go. Captain Teeple will drop you off in Seattle. The boys from Fort Lewis weathered it pretty good there, they have a pretty large safe zone, and General Antico is in charge. He has been briefed, and will be waiting to get you guys geared up for your trek back to Cheyenne. The bad news is that all of our aviation assets are tied up right now as we are airlifting survivors to safe zones that we have set up across the U.S. Right now the plan is to get as many survivors as we can to places where we can make a stand. You will be briefed more when you guys make it back here, but you will be going cross-country from Fort Lewis to Cheyenne. General Antico has some assets for you that will help out, and I think that some of them may even be to your liking. We will talk when you are on Terra Firma tomorrow and then get you guys heading back this way."

The rest of the night was spent with the team packing up their gear, getting prepped to move out, loading weapons, cross-loading equipment and getting things replaced that they had lost along the way. Doctor Lyons told Opie that he planned on staying with the ship, and that when they went up to Anchorage he was going to stay there and try to start over again. He told him that Captain Teeple would be doing runs from coast to coast to try and get survivors, and that he would have a place in the military in Alaska. They spent the evening together with Moon talking about their families and about old times.

The Skipper, Meat and Achilles all had dinner together. The Skipper said it was an old naval tradition for officers to eat their meals together, and since all of this had happened, he hadn't done much of this sort of thing. Achilles told him about his father being on Tybee Island, and said that if the Chung Hoon ever made it to the Atlantic his dad wouldn't be hard to find. He told the Skipper proudly that his dad was an old Army officer and was sure that he was out there surviving and trying to help others.

Chapter 18

Back in the USA

The Port of Seattle was monstrous, and after the team got a good look at it, there was no question as to why it had become a safe zone. The people had organized with the government, and moved sea-land vans or cargo containers along the roads and created a virtual wall that the Z's couldn't get through. Another thing that was pretty astonishing was the sheer amount of people. There were a number of naval vessels, commercial ships, fishing ships, and people who had yachts in the harbor. The Chung Hoon came into port and the team wished everyone farewell. The Skipper went over to Achilles and handed him a nickel plated .45 caliber pistol.

"My father was a sailor, as was his father before him; this pistol was given to my grandfather by General MacArthur himself. I know it is flashy, but I know of no other officer to give it to whom has done so much for this nation."

Achilles tried to give him the weapon back but the Skipper would have nothing to do with it. They said their goodbyes to each other gravely, with standard salutes and then a big bear hug, and then walked down the gangway.

At the bottom they were met by two men that Achilles knew. He almost fell over when he saw who they were. 1LT Ryne "B" BeMiller and 1SG Dave "Mac" Long had both been members of Achilles' DELTA team when he got hurt in Afghanistan. Hugs and handshakes were exchanged, and they loaded up all of their gear in the back of an old Army Deuce and Half (otherwise known as a 2 ½ ton truck).

On the ride to meet with Gen. Antico, B and Mac told Achilles about their last three and a half years. They had been at Fort Lewis training when the shit hit the fan, and had been assigned to help with security and rescue missions since they had been here. They both lost their families, and knew the same thing had happened to everyone on the team. They spent the ride talking and shooting the breeze, giving Achilles hell about his rank and how "buff" he looked. He told them that maybe he could let them know more about it, and he hoped that they would be part of the briefing. They spent the rest of the ride quietly, while the team noticed that their senses all seemed to be heightened, or to be better explained, enhanced.

They came to a halt at the headquarters building at Fort Lewis. People seemed to be in a lax state, and security didn't seem to be anything out of the ordinary. There were armed guards wearing appropriate uniforms and that made the team proud. Outside of what they had seen at Cheyenne and Fort Carson, this was the only other version of a functioning military that they had come across during their travels. They did notice that there were crops planted inside the base's grounds, and the storage containers forming protective barricades against the Z's were as far as the eye could see. Moon realized that he could see so much better now that he could actually see people walking the perimeter of the cargo containers over three miles away. With the naked eye, that was pretty amazing. He shook his head in disbelief.

As they were dismounting the Deuce and a Half, the General came out to meet with them. Achilles called the group to attention and they saluted the General as a unit, well, except for Doctor Baker who looked like SGT Bilko saluting a commander. The General invited the team in, had two aides come out and get their gear, and told them that they would be bunked to prepare for their follow on mission back to Cheyenne. General Antico assured the team that their gear would be good to go, and they let the aides take it all except for the case that Opie would not let anyone else handle.

The team followed the General to the briefing room and he asked them to all take a seat. Achilles noticed that B and Mac stayed with them, but knew that it would be explained during the briefing that was to come.

"Gentlemen," said the General. "Honcho and I have been in extensive contact since you men left on your vital mission. First, let me thank you and tell you how much this means for our nation and indeed for all humanity."

The team all nodded solemnly in acknowledgment.

The next step is getting you guys back to Cheyenne so that Doctor Baker and his team can get to work on a vaccine and whatever research they can get from the data and specimens that you brought back with you. Honcho wanted me to give you a rundown of how things are, and what the current state of things in the U.S. and abroad are looking like. Our first plan is starting here and at Lake Michigan. We are taking these containers and creating a safe zone North of that line. We estimate that maybe 3-5% of the population of the U.S., and roughly 25% of the Canadian population is unaffected. We know that the Zombies are slower in the cold, and that they freeze and can be killed rather easily when it is winter. We are creating another safe zone in Florida starting in the Keys. We will then go east along the Great Lakes and basically try to make all of Canada a free and safe zone. The U.S. and Canadian governments are working together to make it one place safe for everyone. Most of the islands are safe, but we have written off mainland Central and South America, Australia, most of Europe and Southern Asia. We are working together to get the government back and running, and to consolidate all of our forces."

The team looked at the map and they all seemed to be impressed. By the looks of this, the government had been at work on this project for some time, just kind of seemed funny that no one had mentioned it to the team prior to them getting sent to North Korea. Achilles thought about it and it made sense: hide the fact that a safe zone was being created, but use the asset to its best ability.

General Antico went on with his briefing. "There are a number of survival groups that have banded together, it is kind of like the Wild West outside of the wire. We have little air support, and at this point we cannot fly you back to Cheyenne. That is the reason that Mac and B are here with us, Honcho said that you may need another member or two for your team, and since you have served together, I figured they would be a good fit. The plan for now is to get you guys two trucks, as much gear and supplies as you can carry, and send you on your way. You will have Predator coverage for most of each day, and of course you will be in communications with Cheyenne once you guys are on the road. Some good news, the scientists at Cheyenne have actually gotten enough satellites back into the correct orbits that we can now have better access to things. Most of your journey is through what we are considering Indian Country now, it was pretty much out of the EMP blasts so if you have to requisition a vehicle, well then you know what to do. Gentlemen, you have two days to get refit, squared away, and then we expect you on the road. Mac will take you to your billeting, and he and B have the documentation that you need to get gear and supplies."

With that the General wished them good luck, mentioned that he needed to get back to work supervising the ditch they were building, and told the team that if there was anything else they needed to let him know as it would be treated with the highest priority.

B and Mac led them to a building a few hundred meters away, and they found all of their gear inside. It was a generous enough place, and the team took a few minutes to talk about things and to get a plan in action. B and Mac said they were leaving and would be back with their gear within the hour.

Achilles started the conversation. "Do you guys feel the same way I do? I mean, I can see and hear better than ever in my life, and I generally feel better physically."

The entire team agreed that they felt the same way.

Doctor Baker said, "I think our bodies were mutated on a molecular level due to the combination of what the North Koreans had in the vial and what we had from Cheyenne. I don't know how, but whatever the astronauts brought back with them, it changed us."

Achilles thought for a moment and then started issuing orders. "First things first, let's get out a map and plan a route. Woody, that's what you will be doing. Moon, you and Meat go to the motor pool and get a look at those two vehicles. Big Brown, you and Opie go to the ammo depot and get us anything that you think we'll need. Big Joe, I want you to go to the gym, see what kind of weight you can lift, and let me know if you think you are any stronger. Run and see if you get winded, you know, basically go and do some PT and let me know how you feel afterwards. Those results will be useful for the doctors here on staff. Doc, you and I are going to wait for Mac and B and let them know how we are feeling, and hopefully we can make some sense out of all of this. You guys know what to do, it's 1230 hours, let's reconvene for chow at 1700 then get to work with loading the trucks. I want to be out of here in less than three days. Any questions?"

No one had any questions, and they all went on their way.

Meat and Moon stepped out and asked one of the guards which way to the motor pool. A young PFC named Saucier volunteered to take them to it. There were four guards outside, and they told the team members that they were basically there to help the team around and to get them anything that they needed. They all got in a golf cart and took the mile ride out to the motor pool.

At the motor pool the young Private escorted them to the main office. Inside was a man sitting down and poring over paperwork. "Hey are you guys the team"? he asked, and Meat nodded in the affirmative.

"All right then, the old man told me to get you guys saddled up and ready to move. I've been thinking about what your team would need. We don't have anything huge, but we have converted a few things here and there. I think you may like what I have in store. By the way, the name's Baron, Baron Snydor.

Mr. Snydor, or the Baron as he liked to refer to himself, walked them through the motor pool. There was quite a collection of everything from pickup trucks to SUVs to cars, and of course the usual assortment of military vehicles.

Baron stopped at a clamshell (a temporary storage unit maintenance garage) and fumbled with his keys to open the door. "Listen up, brothers, these two vehicles are the finest things that I have. My guys have been working on them for a while, and we were going to use them for long-range reconnaissance, but the man says they are all yours now."

They entered the facility and he turned on the lights. As soon as they saw the vehicles, they both knew what they were, or at least what they used to be.

"These here beauties are the Baron Specials. They are up-armored, with extended fuel capacities and storage units, and we have put the frames on so that none of those pesky biters can take a chunk out of you."

Meat and Moon had both seen the RSOVs (Ranger Special Operations Vehicles) in action before. They were modified Land Rovers set up for all kinds of operations.

The Baron went on. "Each one can run for 500 miles without refueling; there is a mount on the top for .50 calibers or M-240's, and plenty of extra room in the back. Run flat tires, and we will have a dirt bike strapped to the back of each one. I will have them ready and delivered to your place in the morning."

With that, Moon and Meat thanked him for his help, and then they went back toward their billet.

As they were on the way back, they saw a large civilian box truck pull up outside of the house that they were staying at, and Big Brown and Opie climbed out of the back. They had been to the ammo depot and picked up enough firepower to level a small city. They had gotten enough ammo for all of the weapons. They would need to go back to get .50 calibers, but they were unsure if they would need them depending on the transportation. They got claymores, fragmentation and incendiary grenades, and a few other ins- and outs.

When most of the team had returned and were putting all of the new gear inside with the help of the guards that were there to keep the crowd to a minimum, they saw that Stewy and Achilles were talking things over with Mac and B. They went about their business and knew that when Achilles was ready, he would get all of them together.

"Basically, guys, we are supposedly immune to the virus. So on this journey back to Cheyenne, I want you guys to drive. If we need to clear a building, check something out, or whatever, I would rather you guys be safe than dead; you'll stay with the transport. We know that a bite will no longer infect us, but that still doesn't mean that we cannot be ripped to shreds. Still, I would feel better knowing that if you get bit that I won't have to do the inevitable." B and Mac both knew the deal, they were experienced in their own regard. They still looked a little skeptical but Achilles knew that they had been briefed and that they were smart and experienced enough to trust the intelligence reports that they had seen.

Achilles got the team together and asked a simple question: "What do we have?" The team settled in at a table to discuss how they would be going about the next part of their mission.

Hollywood started. "OK, guys, here are the basic's of the route that we will be taking. There isn't much of a straight route for us to take, but we will be covering a good part of the American West. We will try to stick to the main state roads. We will go through a lot of State parks, and that way we can stay off of the highways. From the intel that I have gathered, there are a lot of dead vehicles on the roads.

Dead vehicles equal the possibility of running into packs of undead, possibly some trapped in cars and such. I feel that this is our best possible route to get us back to Cheyenne. I have spoken to the G-2 "Intelligence" and he will make sure that we have Predator coverage for most of the trip."

Achilles gave him a nod, and the team looked over the map. They would come into contact with many small towns, but would try to stay away from the larger areas. Large areas equaled large gatherings of zombies. He couldn't help but notice that the route took them by many airfields on the way. "Woody, I see a lot of airfields, do you care to enlighten us on your thinking?"

"No worries," said Woody. "I thought that the ability to have safe places to sleep as being a plus. Moving at night may be a little treacherous due to shamblers or walkers being in the road, and also the other things we could run into make that pretty bad. Airfields and State parks give us the opportunity to come across places that we can secure rather easily. Also, we may have the opportunity to requisition another aircraft."

"Very good, that is good thinking. Opie, what did you and Big Brown come up with?"

"Ok, guys, we are refit, all of our weapons except for crew serve and vehicle mounted weapons are silenced. We all have our M-4's, we have enough ammo that we shouldn't have any worries. I got a .50 cal for one vehicle, and we have an M-240 for the other. We have enough batteries, grenades, claymores, Laws, and MREs to be self-sufficient. We now have two Barretts, and four M-24's that are silenced. We just need the vehicles to get them cross-loaded and prepped to move out."

Achilles took a look over the inventory list and gave out a little whistle. "Good job fellas, I think that we are actually outfitted better than any of the previous legs of our mission. Vehicle One will have B driving, Moon, Big Brown, Big Joe in the turret, and me. Vehicle Two will have Mac driving, Meat, Woody, and Doc Baker. If we draw contact, at all costs B, Mac, and Doc Baker are to stay in the vehicles. I do not want anything to happen to you guys. I know that Doc Baker is like us, but these godless bastards can still rip him apart. I really like the fact that we have bigger guns, but we will not use them unless we really need them. I don't want to be heard from miles away. Speaking of vehicles, Meat, what did you guys come up with?"

"OK gentlemen, we have requisitioned a few RSOVs or Ranger Special Operations Vehicles. They have been modified. The lead vehicle has a V-shaped plow on it, and they have been up-armored. They are essentially silent, and we have a bike mounted on the back for recon work. The guy who modified them is unique to say the least, but he has these babies ready to go. We also have some fuel additives that we can use to siphon gas and make it useable again. We will have the vehicles in the morning, and we should be able to get them ready to go."

Achilles nodded in approval. "OK guys, let's get some chow. Meat and Woody are with me. We have to go see General Antico and have a meeting with Honcho." The team broke, knowing they would reconvene at 2200 hours.

Chapter 19

Final Preparations

Achilles went to the meeting with General Antico with Meat and Woody in tow. As they entered the room, they found the General had a few people with him at the meeting. To their great surprise, they encountered a person from their not so long ago past. General Antico made the introductions that were not needed. "Gentlemen, I was briefed that you already knew one another, but this is Agent Madam." They said hello, and were surprised when she hugged each member of the team and thanked them for what they had done since they were essentially lost in the second jump.

She spent a few moments going over what she knew about the situation and explaining that she was here when everything went to shit. She also stepped up to the map and let the team know about the efforts of the U.S. and Canadian governments and the building of the wall. General Antico also spent time explaining about the wall, the checkpoints that they were building every hundred or so miles, and the need for the team to get the results of their exploits back into the hands of the researchers at Cheyenne Mountain.

"Col. Achilles. I have been reading the reports of the experimental cure that you and your team inoculated yourselves with. Let me say that this is groundbreaking, and I commend your team for making the group decision that led to you men still being alive. I am interested in the aftereffects of what happened to your bimolecular makeup and the changes that you gentlemen are experiencing. What have you found out so far, and can you feel the difference?" The Madam had just asked the one hundred dollar question.

Achilles began. "Ma'am, we all know that we are hungrier, this would possibly be due to having an increased metabolism; we can see and hear better than ever, and seem to have all of our senses heightened. We appear to be a whole lot stronger, and are yet to know if our combat skills are heightened. I am sure that when we get back to Cheyenne they will poke and prod us and do all sorts of testing to figure out if we are affected in any other way."

At that point the monitor on the wall came alive, and Honcho and Eagle were present for the briefing. Pleasantries were exchanged, and Honcho gave them all a quick update on what was going on in their neck of the woods

154

so to speak. Eagle spoke to the team also. He congratulated them all on their success and commended them on how well they had done.

Honcho spent the next bit of time discussing the ongoing missions with the state of the former nation, and the wall. He also told the team about the bombs loaded with gas that they were hoping would neutralize the zombies, but they were not making a lot of headway in that department. He then asked about the route and timeline that Achilles and the team had put together.

Achilles started. "Sir, we are going to take a southeastern route. We will stay off of main routes and try to avoid large danger areas and the possibility of hoards of the walkers. We plan on using airports, State parks, and any structures that we can secure to sleep and provide rest points during our journey. We plan on also trying to locate anything that can speed up the trip, possibly finding an airplane or helicopter that Hollywood can operate. We have coordinated to have Predator support for almost the entire trip, it seems the boys back at Cheyenne have the satellites operating better. We are going to strike out tomorrow morning at 0900 local; we will be using modified RSOVs to move out. The motor pool here has modified them with armor and they can be sealed up in case we encounter a hoard. We are armed and ready to go, we have added two team members and they have worked with me in the past. We will make communication checks with you every twelve hours: 0900 and 2100, and if we miss two checks we should be considered compromised. We have been briefed about the missions that are ongoing with the aviation assets, and we know we are essentially on our own. We have uploaded a schematic of the route to the S-2 (Intelligence Section) at Cheyenne and they should be able to account for our general whereabouts."

Honcho and Eagle both were impressed with what they heard. They knew that the team was good at their job, and secretly were relieved that they had ended up in this time. The fact was that they were put together way back when because they had been studied and analyzed for years prior to putting the team together. The unique skill sets that each member had were actually put into motion by school selections while in the service, prodding from the intel community that had guided them through friendships in the military, and it had all been set up by the Madam. She and the

Secretary had been working on this project for almost ten years. This went as far back as Honcho's father. He had been a member of the CIA, and unbeknownst to his own son had guided him, mentored, and prepared him for West Point, Ranger School, Special Forces Selection, Combat Dive School, and being a DELTA Team Leader. His father had been an operative and even had training with the famous SAS (Special Air Service) of Great Britain. All of this went through Honcho's mind in a flash.

Finally the meeting concluded. Eagle gave one final "good luck" to the team and the uplink ended. The team spent the rest of the evening dining with the General, and talking about old times with each other. General Antico spoke in length about the building of the wall; he told them how they were going up and down the West Coast all the way to the Panama Canal to get the shipping containers to compose the wall. He gave them a rundown of what was thought to be left of humanity, the numbers that the three officers heard were staggering. He went on to discuss the continued rescue of survivor groups, and the sheer vastness of the task of providing for and protecting the base. They finished up their meal and the team said their goodbyes to the General and his staff.

As the team was walking back to the building that they were staying at, Achilles noticed how far he could see in the dark, and also the detail in which he could do so. He thought about it and asked Meat and Woody if they could see that well also. It turned out that they all could see that well. It wasn't as good as night vision devices, but they could see at least ten times better and with more detail than ever before. This would be another thing to tell the scientists at Cheyenne about the mutations from the serum.

Just then, a Sergeant approached the group from behind as a jog. He saluted the Col. and asked that they return to the General's headquarters building. He did not know what was so important, but did tell them that a gentleman had come to see General Antico and the General had sent him to get the team back to his headquarters immediately.

The team headed back toward the headquarters building; they had no clue as to what was going on, but everything seemed to be normal, and this type of thing can and does happen in the military. They got back to the building and they were escorted directly to the General's briefing room that they had just left.

Inside was the man that they had met earlier: Baron Snydor. He was there briefing the General about the vehicles that his team was getting ready for Achilles' team to move across the country in. "Listen up brothers, the RSOVs are a no go. We cannot retro fit them with armor in case you guys get into trouble. I do have another solution that we have been working on. They are modified up-armored (HMMWV), these beauties are ready to go, and you can basically wait out the masses of zombies until you run out of food. They are silent, and when I mean silent, they are quieter than a Hybrid was when it ran on batteries. I came back here to discuss it with the boss, and he told me to go ahead and give them up."

Achilles thanked him for the info, and they once again said their good evenings with the General. They headed back to the rest of the team. They needed to do a final back brief prior to retiring for the night, and then they could get some shuteye prior to heading out on the open road. They would need to get updated route data from Cheyenne to see if there were any masses of undead that they would need to try to get around, and then the final weapons and equipment checks prior to loading up.

They finished up with everything and went to bed for the night. They were ready to move, and the past few days had provided the team with a good rest. They had all spoken about how they felt; they seemed to be better versions of themselves and when they were tested in battle Achilles hoped that there wouldn't be any surprises such as fatigue, hunger, thirst, or possibly even having a mental freak out.

Sleep came and went for the team. Some slept better than others, but this was common for most soldiers. At 0700 they were all up and getting their gear ready to head out. They started getting everything out front to load up the vehicles that the Baron had promised would be there promptly at 0730. He was dead on with that time, and both vehicles pulled up with ten seconds left to spare. The lead vehicle had the plow as promised, and the Baron had a huge grin on his face.

Baron spent a little time talking to Meat and B about the extras that were on the vehicle. They were pretty standard, but they could be completely sealed to almost create a Nuclear, Biological, and Chemical (NBC) secure environment. The windows had been tinted, and the front windows had shades that could be pulled down so that they could be completely blacked out. This would help if they had to stop and wait for one of the herds to pass bye.

They thanked him for the work, then got busy loading all the gear in the vehicle. They mounted an M-240 on the front vehicle, and a .50 cal on the second vehicle. All the food and water was split into both vehicles and the same with the ammunition. Communications checks were established with Cheyenne and Fort Lewis. Moon got a rundown of the latest intelligence loaded into the pad devices and synced up their transponder so that they could be located at all times by the brass at the mountain.

As they mounted up and said their farewells to General Antico and his staff, they had no clue that this part of their journey would be their hardest so far. They got under way and drove out of the main gate into the rising sun as they headed southeast toward Colorado and the Cheyenne Mountain complex.

Chapter 20

Back on The Road

The first hour of their drive went by without much fanfare. They made good time because the soldiers and people at Fort Lewis had cleared most of the road at this point. They had used the dead vehicles to create a barrier on both sides of the road. Zombies could still get through, but it was only by literally squeezing or crawling through the barricade. Achilles wondered if they were smart enough to do this, but he was sure in the near future they would find out.

As they drove on they noticed the destruction that the zombies had caused. They had all seen this before, most of the team on the trip to Cheyenne, Doc Baker while he was evacuated during the horrors of the world ending, and the two new members while they fought for the last three years for their lives and to try to keep America together. Homes and neighborhoods had been burned to the ground, stores were looted and destroyed, cars where you could only imagine what had happened to the occupants. Had they struck out on foot, tried to outwait a hoard, run out of gas? The possibilities were endless. Achilles knew that he wasn't the only person that was seeing the destruction, who knows, maybe they were getting numb to it?

The first day went by relatively quietly. The team saw small groups of shamblers walking about, in singles or in pairs, but they drove past without much of an issue. They didn't have to move many vehicles, but when they did they used the plow on the front of Vehicle One while Vehicle Two would provide over watch for them. Around 1500 hours they stopped and did a map check. They talked about the route and they discussed trying to use the secondary roads. They shelved this process for the time being for the sake of time.

They decided to go to the town and get to the Tri-Cities Airport in Pasco. They would get off of the highway and take I-182 until they needed to exit and get to the airport. They briefed what they were planning and then moved out. They had a man in each turret to provide a lookout/spotter for any movement, and the rest of the team was on high alert. This was not a large city by any means, but they knew they could get into trouble quickly. This was change in the way that most of them had operated in the past. Most Special Operations teams learn to love the night and operate under the blanket of security that the darkness provides.

As they pulled off of the highway and followed the signs that led them to the airport, they could see that there had been the same destruction here as everywhere else they had been. Buildings that showed people had holed up in them to make their last stands, and widespread devastation. They made their way to the airport and knew instantly that the terminal would be a bad choice. Just by doing a small recon of the area they could see that there were many undead trapped in the terminal. Achilles thought to himself that this place was never going to be the same. It was the first time that he actually felt that there was no way that his family could have made it through this hellish nightmare.

One good thing, the airport was actually still secure inside of the fence line. They could not see anything moving on the tarmac, and this should make for an easily defended area. When everything had gone down, the TSA had been in charge of any airport that had substantial amounts of travelers. They found the gate to get to the tower after circling most of the airport. Another great thing was that most airports have a perimeter or frontage road around them. They pulled up to the gate and Moon went to work on getting it open. Opie provided security and it only took a moment for Moon to tell Achilles that the gate was electronic and there of course was no security. They solved this issue by hooking up a chain to the second vehicle, pulled the gate open and closed it once they were inside. They used a simple set of zip ties to secure the gate.

They looked out of the vehicles as they made their way across the tarmac; they saw the faces of the undead staring out the windows of the terminal and following their every move. Big Brown spoke up. "Look at those Sucker Heads just staring and watching us." This got a chuckle out of the group. They approached the tower and of course knew they would have to clear it to make sure it was secure. There were good and bad issues with using air-traffic control towers as a place to hole up. First, they were almost the best place to defend themselves. The windows were always darkened so that they wouldn't be able to be seen from the outside, and they could clear it easier than most of the other structures. The main fall back to this was the fact that they could get surrounded and not be able to get away. This was a chance that the team would have to take. It was too far to make it to any other airfield or possibly a rest stop or state park that had a building made of brick or stone.

They pulled the HMMWVs to the front of the tower and faced them both out at a 45 degree angles. This way they could provide over watch and overlapping fields of fire from the crew served or mounted weapons on the vehicles. It seemed secure to the team, but they didn't know if there were any crawlers or if the zombies had gotten any smarter, even though this seemed to be way more of a fantasy to Achilles. The team got out of the vehicles and provided security so that they could be assigned tasks. The tower appeared to be three stories high, and it would take most of the team to secure it. Achilles knew this fact, but he wanted it done quietly and wasn't sure yet how the mutation might affect them in battle.

They rounded up and Achilles had B and Mac stay on the turrets; they were only to observe and if there was trouble they were to get back inside and wait for further orders. They attached silencers to their Heckler &

Koch .45 calibers and all donned their night vision devices to be able to put them on if the lighting was bad. They stacked on the door and Opie used the lock pick set to open it up. It was locked and they wanted to be able to secure it for the night. Opie took a moment to open the door and they entered the tower. As soon as the team was in they closed the door and could already see the amount of dust that had accumulated inside. The ground floor was secure and the elevator was stuck open. It wouldn't operate anyway without power, and a quick sweep of it showed that there was nothing inside of it. The team continued up the stairs until they reached the second story. It was definitely goggle dark inside. The door to the upper part of the tower must have been closed, therefore the only light was from the sliver that penetrated under the door on the ground level.

Big Brown and the Doc were told to remain in place and to cover the stairs. They nodded and at this point Achilles knew that they would do what he expected of them. To be honest, Achilles had no clue as to how Big Brown would react when he once again came face to face with the undead. It had only been three weeks since Little Brown had been decapitated and they had buried him at sea. Big

Brown had lost his entire family to the Zombies and there had to be some rage built inside of him. On the outside he was a steel trap, never getting emotional and shedding few tears after the death of his eldest son. For this reason it was Achilles' decision not to put him up front while he was in charge of this team. He would definitely get him to a shrink when they got back to Cheyenne, but knew that he could never let this man not be part of the team. To take that away at this point would probably be the final blow to Big Brown's psyche.

Meat was in front and he and Opie cracked two Infra Red chemical lights and threw them out in both directions on the landing. This was the only wide part that was in the tower. They split left and right and looked down the second floor. A quick recon of the area showed that it was clear, they had already figured this out since there was no smell, but this team was not going to become complacent and take those kinds of chances. In Ranger School, which most of them had attended, they were taught – actually it was drilled into their heads - that complacency kills.

The next flight took them to the top of the tower. The door was secured and Moon

168

used a fiber optic cable that he was able to slip under the door to check the inside. He told the team it appeared to be clear, and there was only one blind spot to the right. Normally a team like this would use a dynamic entry tactic and toss a flash bang grenade inside to disorient and confuse an enemy. The main problem with using this approach here was that they didn't know if it would work on Zombies. Moon then checked the door handle and it turned freely. They burst in and to their surprise again it was clear. It looked as if someone had left in a hurry, but there were no undead or even dead bodies in the upper level.

Achilles called the all clear and told the team to join them up top. They would get food and water inside, and secure the door at the bottom for the remainder of the day and hole up until the sun came up. They each located a spot on the floor where they would spend the night and got their gear set up so that they could settle in for the night. They made contact with Fort Lewis and got them to relay their position and situation to Cheyenne, and they were told that they would have Predator assets available to them for the next five hours. At that point they would be on their own until around 0917 local time in the morning.

Achilles looked out the window with Meat standing by his side. They both just stared, as they knew that they couldn't be seen inside of the tower by watching eyes below. The big question was whether their scent would attract any of the undead to their location. They were not sure how much of the Zombies' senses remained from when they were alive, but at times they seemed to be able to smell a human at great distances. There was an access hatch to the top of the tower; Achilles told the team that he wanted a man up all night in one hour shifts. Big Brown and Dr. Baker would have the 0200-0300 shift and would pull it together. They would man it come nighttime, and there would be no light just in case they could be seen outside.

Achilles had drawn the 0300-0400 duty, he was the leader and knew that the men respected him because he was just as much part of the detail as the rest of them. They all ate and spoke about things from their past. Mac even astonished them all by telling them his survival story and how he ended up being at Fort Lewis.

Mac was originally from Bend, Oregon. His father was a logger and tried to do what he could to get his son to get out of Oregon.

Following his advice, Mac enlisted in the Army to be an Airborne Ranger and had progressed through the ranks. He went through Pathfinder, Combat Diver, and eventually became a Special Forces Demolitions Specialist. He had worked with Achilles in the past when their two teams in Delta were both working in Afghanistan. He had been in for 17 years and loved being a soldier. He had just rotated back to the States and was on leave when the bombs fell. He saw walkers take down his family, and barely escaped with his own life. For the next month he walked cross-country, scavenging for himself. He carried a heavy load of guilt that he was unable to protect his mother, father, and sister from this hell on earth. He carried demons just like the rest of the men and woman that were now part of this new world. He told the team about his journey and the many occasions he had nearly been killed. He eventually made it to Fort Lewis as they were reorganizing and now did everything he could to try to kill as many of the walker bastards as he could.

The team listened and nodded and looked down at their feet during the story. They all knew that everyone that had experienced the apocalypse had a similar tale to tell. The original members of the team could only hope that in some way they still had someone out there. They all knew that the man next to them was thinking the same thing. That was when B asked Achilles what the team's story was.

Achilles looked at the other members and thought to himself, why the hell not tell these guys what their story was. After taking a little while to fill them in about the program, the time travel and their perilous journey across the country, he told them about their link up with the government at Cheyenne Mountain, the follow on mission, meeting up with Big Brown and his son, the ship, Wake Island, Korea, and their journey back. It seemed that B and Mac were more stunned than when Mac was telling his own story.

That was when Big Brown chimed in. "You mean to tell me that you guys are from the past? I call Bullshit!" He slapped his hand on his knee and said if it was true that he would "suck a fat baby's dick."

That was when Moon showed them everything via the PAD; they were all stunned. Woody spoke up and made a comment about Big Brown being true to his word and actually doing what he said, that got a laugh out of the entire group.

They got ready for the night as darkness approached. The Zombies seemed to be more on alert and even hungrier during the night time, and seemed to be blinded or a little disoriented during the daytime. At night was when the Runners came out to hunt. They all knew this, but felt at least relatively safe since they were in a tower with no way for the Zombies to get in. The only real question was how they would egress from the tower and the airfield if they were discovered.

As they settled in to get some shuteye, the radio came to life with a sitrep (Situation Report) of the area that the intelligence people had gathered by taking pictures with the drones.

"Seeker Element, Cheyenne has sitrep following, prepare to copy… Large horde advancing from the south in your general direction, best guess is ten to twenty thousand in the group. They are advancing at a slow pace but they are only 10 kilometers from your location, south by southwest. S-2 Element advises waiting until they pass your location or find an alternate route away from the area…

."Then the message repeated itself two more times and the radio went silent.

Achilles was glad that Mac had brought the laser designator into the tower. He took it topside to Hollywood and told him what the situation was. If they saw a large group and if they were heading in their general direction they needed to stay quiet. They wouldn't have Predator coverage until 0900 hours local, but they needed this piece of equipment to paint the target if they needed it. Since movement attracted attention, it was better to move the designator up there now in case they needed it in the morning.

The team settled in and they all eventually got to sleep. Time went by and Achilles was woken up for his watch by Big Brown as he and Doc Baker were coming back down. As he climbed topside he was a little shocked by the clarity of the sky. He knew that it would be clear, but in this darkness he could see every star in the sky.

He was almost done with his shift when he heard the first screams of the runners. He wasn't sure if it was a scream or more of a guttural howling that enabled all the others to converge on their position. They seemed to be almost leading the other zombies in this manner. He raised his goggles and just south of the airport he could see the masses of undead heading in their general direction. He silently slipped back into the tower and woke up the rest of the team so that they could gather and store everything just in case all hell broke loose.

Everyone got up and did what they needed to do. It was almost surreal looking out the windows and seeing what looked like a tidal wave of darkness moving across the landscape and coming their way. They spoke in hushed tones and geared up. Meat and Woody went downstairs and positioned themselves just in case there were some zombies that might try to check out the tower. This was highly unlikely, but they knew better than to think they were safe. Achilles looked at his watch and knew that sunrise was in an hour and a half. They would probably have to spend a majority of the day in the tower since the zombies would take their sweet ass time going around the airfield, and the fact that they might start to just mill about with the sunrise coming.

After an hour or so the sun started to rise. The good thing was that the horde walked around the fence to the airport; the bad part was that they stopped just to the north and looked like a herd of cattle milling about. The team spoke about what to do. It was Mac that came up with an idea that they would need to speak to Cheyenne about. He told the team that they should use a Predator to take out a building north of them. That would get the Runners all in a tizzy and the shamblers would do their part and fall in to investigate the explosion. That should buy them enough time to get back out and on the road. They would have to wait until 0900 to have a Predator on station, and then they would need to be ready to move out.

Chapter 21

No Support

They checked in with Fort Lewis and got their relay to Cheyenne. The news was not good from the get go. Both of the Predators that supported the team were not going to be airborne today. They were both down for parts. This was a problem that they had all been through before, and knew that they would probably have to deal with again. The problem here was that this was going to delay the team even longer from getting back. To compound the delay, there was a blanket of fog over the entire area, low pressure was coming in and the weather was going to take a turn for the worse.

They all talked about the situation. They knew that they would be there for at least another twenty-four to forty-eight hours due to weather, and moving without air support was just stupid. The Predators had saved their collective fourth points of contacts prior to getting on the ship, and they all knew that the man and woman that operated them were worth their weight in gold.

They had a couple of options: they could launch a flare over the heads of the undead to draw their attention, and possibly get out that way, but if there were any runners milling around it could turn into sheer chaos. They had brought in close to four days' worth of food and water so that wasn't going to be a problem; they could use the toilet until they couldn't fill it up anymore, and they would start to get the smell of shit and piss prior to running out food. They tossed a few ideas around and decided it was best to stay put. They would have to make another hole in the fence, and that would make the airfield's ability to remain relatively secure a lost cause. They all knew that other travelers would probably try this same tactic sometime in the future.

The team consulted the map. They planned on pushing through to just outside of Baker City, Oregon. Woody had a state park circled on the map as their next stopping point. It should have some sort of lodge or something that they could secure, or they would try to find an area that had a building that they could hole up in for the night. As they were studying the map it was Big Brown that alerted the team to what was going on outside. The fog had started to clear and the undead were right outside the fence. The most alarming part that made his skin crawl, and affected the others just as strongly, was that the undead were looking right at the tower. The team knew there was no way that they could be seen through the darkened glass of the tower, but it seemed that they were being watched closely and that the undead knew that they were inside.

Dr. Baker spoke up and mentioned that from what they had studied of the zombies, they knew one thing for sure: they could smell really well. In fact, the team had noticed that their sense of smell seemed to be heightened. Dr. Baker went on to talk about the studies that he had been part of prior to the beginning of the mission. The zombies were more docile during the day, seemingly almost blinded by the sun, but if there was movement they could follow it. The other interesting fact was that the runners didn't seem to be as affected by the elements as the shamblers were.

Achilles took it all in. He didn't want this tower to be his final resting place. If they started to push for the fence they would have to beat feet out of the area. They would have to make an opening in the fence which would leave this place harder to secure in the future. It was finally hitting him that the only place that they could actually secure would be the upper regions that the government was working on in Canada. This realization drove home to him that he would probably never see his family again, even if they had made it through all this shit. He struggled with himself to push those emotions back into that dark place. He had to keep that hope alive, if not, was life still worth living? For hundreds of years soldiers had fought for things that they didn't believe in - they fought to protect their loved ones, and this time would be no different.

The team waited and watched. The undead never seemed to take their eyes (or what was left of them) off of the tower. The only good news was that the team could probably load the Hummers up and get moving prior to the herd seeing them move out. They had parked next to the tower on the opposite side of the fence. They were all glad for that now. They began working on a contingency plan just in case the masses started to move to the tower. Opie started rigging a device to blow the fence, that way they wouldn't risk destroying or possibly rendering one of the Hummers inoperable. They would then take the back roads to get south of the area and back onto the highway if at all possible. They wouldn't fire unless they had to, as gunfire drew the undead like flies to cow shit and they all knew this. As they were finalizing the plan Big Brown called out that they needed to move, and needed to move now. They looked up and the undead were pushing on the fence. There were way too many to hold off in a sustained firefight, and if they got trapped the zombies would wait them out. The situation went from bad to worse in a heartbeat.

The team hurried down the tower and got into the vehicles. They could hear the moaning and screams of the undead. They took off across the tarmac, and from the turrets Moon and Woody could see the fence start to come down under the sheer weight of the undead pushing on it. Everyone's pucker factor went up a notch. They sped across the airfield and drove straight at the fence line. The runners were the first to clear the fence and were heading directly for the team. They had a good mile lead on them, and by no means were the zombies Olympic runners, but their time would be limited.

Opie was out and moving quickly. He had rigged the charge and was placing it when he heard the first of the runners screaming. It sent chills down his spine. He knew he had plenty of time, but it still made him move in a manner that was quicker than normal. He placed the charge and moved back to the safety of the vehicle. He hit the remote detonator and the fence blew. The hole that was left was big enough for them to drive through, and they moved out as fast as possible. They would have to keep the pace up to get far enough away that the herd of undead would lose the scent of the trucks and that of the team.

The side streets that they were forced to take were clogged and moving was slow. They had to keep driving around dead vehicles and scattered remains of the people that hadn't made it. The only fortunate thing was that they were moving south, and most of the zombies that would have been in the area followed the northbound herd.

They made their way back to the highway and continued south. They would have to keep moving because in the back of their minds they knew that the herd would follow them no matter what. They would be much quicker, but the herd and the hunger for human flesh would keep the zombies moving after them. They would need to scrap their plan and travel as far as possible, since they all knew that distance would be the best thing for them at this point.

As the day wore on the team continued to move in a southwestern direction. Town after town that they saw go by was another example of destruction. The herd that they encountered was probably part of the destruction, and had most likely moved through here looking for more humans to feed upon. The highway showed signs of gridlock near towns, but for the most part those were the only places where there seemed to be a pile up of vehicles. As the day passed Achilles realized that it was coming up on time to find a place for the night. They had rethought their original theory and would try to stay as close to the road as possible. The best-case scenario was to find a brick and mortar type facility, something that was easily defendable and where hasty egress would be possible.

It was B that came up with a bright idea. "How about a rest area? They are usually made of bricks, and we can lock the doors. If we had to, we could probably get through the roof, and they have access in both directions. If you think about it, they are mostly near a wooded area, and that way there shouldn't be open avenues of approach." They had passed a few places like this along the way; it made sense, they should be able to clear the facilities easily, and they should be able to secure them. They would be easy to access from the roads, and they could get moving quickly if need be. Achilles and the rest of the team were pretty happy with that, it made perfect sense, and the only open areas would be the road.

It was close to 1500 hours local time. They would need the daylight to scout and secure the building. The next rest area they came to was rather small, one building and a small area where there used to be a place to get sodas and snacks. The machines had long ago been raided and were actually lying on their sides. From a tactical standpoint, the best part about the rest area was that there was only one entry point at the front of the building. Some of these facilities had entries at the front and back, the parking lot in the front for cars and SUVs, and the 18- wheelers and recreational vehicles and such parking out back. That meant that the team would only have to secure the front of the building and could park the Hummers close and facing out for a hasty getaway if needs be.

They pulled up and immediately went into action. They would need to provide security outside, and the rest of the team would go inside and clear the two bathrooms and any offices. B and Mac manned the turrets in the Hummers, and the rest of the team went inside. Big Brown and the Doc were left at the front door to watch their backs when they went inside the bathrooms. Achilles and Moon took the ladies' room, Meat and Woody took the men's room. The only thing that seemed out of place was the lack of noise that would normally accompany a rest area. There was no smell of death, and no signs of blood or anything out of the ordinary. The ladies' room was cleared and nothing was out of place. Meat nearly shot a squirrel that had made its home inside of the men's room when it came out and scared him half to death. After some laughing and chiding of him, the team then cleared the manager's office.

Once they were done, they backed the vehicles up and placed them nose-to-nose so that they would provide another barrier to the glass front doors of the visitor's center. They moved water and food inside along with the gear that they would need for the night. Achilles got ready to check in with Cheyenne and to determine when they would have Big Brother back airborne to scout and provide that safety net of laser guided missiles to help them out of a jam. They had about two hours before the communications window would open up, so they decided it was a good time to take out the bikes for a recon mission. Meat and Opie would go ahead for an hour and look for signs of survivors or any signs of the undead. They needed to stay in contact every quarter hour and Achilles told them to be back by 1830 hours.

That would give them enough time to secure the bikes and lock the place down for the night.

They were outside of Caldwell, Idaho, or at least what used to be Caldwell. Achilles wanted them to get as close to the outskirts of Boise as they could, since that would be the first big city that they would need to go around. The larger the city, the bigger the threat of masses of undead. From what they had been briefed on while they were at Cheyenne, most people had fled the large cities during the outbreak. As far as the government was concerned, they were dead zones.

The motorcycles were called IMINT's; they were Christini dirt bikes. Rangers and other special operations types used them in Afghanistan prior to this, and they were quick, resilient, and the best part, extremely quiet. It took two team members each to lift them off of the mounts that the Baron had used to mount them. They were secured by cargo straps and came off in a very efficient manner.

Meat and Opie took off after a communications check was made. They were using their PAD devices and would have coverage for close to 20 miles. They each took water and their packs; they knew that being complacent would get them killed. Also, they both had experience on motorcycles and were the best choice to carry out the reconnaissance. They had 2-½ hours to get out there to try to find out what lay ahead for the team.

Achilles made contact with Honcho and got an update of the situation from the top. Honcho said, "You men need to be prepared to make it back here without the Predator support. We have a large herd that we are dealing with outside of Fort Lewis, they are most probably the ones that you came across last night at the airfield. The leading element of them will be there as early as 1200 hours tomorrow. We cannot let that base fall. They are prepping for combat and need to keep it operating at all costs. All of our aviation assets have been diverted that way. We have a no shit situation getting ready to go down in that area. The best thing that you guys have going for you is stealth and your training. We know that there are some communities along your path that have made it this long, and if you have to, try to make it to one of them. That information will be downloaded to your PAD as we are speaking. Colonel, you are in Indian Country now, do what you can to bring your team and that research to us, our people need some sort of hope, and you are it." With that Honcho ended the uplink and Achilles broke the news to the group. From this point until they made it back, they were most probably on their own.

Chapter 22

Recon

Meat and Opie were cruising down the highway and made it to the outskirts of Boise. From the looks of it, the devastation hit this area hard. The first thing that they realized was that they would have to go around the area. There was no way that they could get the Hummers through all of the gridlock. They would have to use side roads that took them well around the city proper.

They backtracked to outside of the city, found an exit and stopped at the top to check in with the team. They made their combo check and decided to head south, which would be the fastest way around the city, and would keep them on track with the plan. They at least had the fortune of unplowed or unplanted fields that gave them an unrestricted view of the land. They both knew their best bet would be to try and stay in a radius that would keep them going more east than south, but at this point they were at the mercy of the roads.

Meat was ahead of Opie by about 50 meters, that way if they had to stop and fight Opie could cover Meat while he turned around to withdraw from the situation. This was what was to prove to be the most fortunate thing for the two-man team. The only things that they saw were fields and what used to be smaller subdivisions.

As they approached a subdivision on the south side of the street, Opie saw Meat get thrown forward off of his bike. He flipped through the air and landed on his side. He skidded about 30 feet and it was all that Opie could do to stop without getting taken out himself. Someone had strung a cable across the road about a foot off the ground. Opie tipped off his bike and brought his weapon up. He stayed behind the bike in case someone was watching him, and called out to Meat. Meat was unresponsive to his calls. Opie waited for what seemed like an eternity. To his surprise there were no gun shots, so he moved over to Meat.

Meat had taken a nasty spill and was knocked out cold. The helmet that he was wearing probably saved his life. The left side of his face was skinned up, and his arm looked like it was broken. Opie assessed his injuries and knew that there was no way he would be able to get them both back to the rest area. His first priority would be to get Meat to a building and treat the injury. He moved both of the bikes off of the road and cut down the damn cable that had taken out Meat. He secured both of their packs and did his best to pick up Meat in a fireman's carry without doing any more damage to the injured soldier. The injuries went well beyond what he was trained to do, especially if Meat had a head injury which was more than likely since he was unconscious.

It was a 500 meter march across a field to the outer line of houses in the subdivision. Opie walked straight for it, keeping his weapon up and hoping that the person who strung that line was not looking at him through a sniper's scope. He knew in the back of his mind that people generally didn't trust the government since they were not able to maintain control after the devastation. He hoped that he would be lucky and get Meat somewhere safe where he could look him over better and treat the situation. It was fortunate for Meat that Opie was the medic in the group, and had training beyond what most people in the special operations community had.

He bypassed two houses because they were made of aluminum siding and chose a two-story full brick model. The house also had a backyard with a privacy fence which would make it easier to secure. He laid Meat down and propped him up against the side of the house, placed his weapon in his hands and went to work securing the house. He went to the front door and knocked on it, that way if there was anything inside he would hear it. No sounds of movement came back; his only choice would be to try to break in. Opie didn't want to violate the integrity of the front of the house since that is where most people try to get into a home like this, so he went around back. After a quick check on Meat he opened the fence and went into the backyard. At this point if a dog had survived it would have dug out in search of food by this point, so that didn't worry him, even though in the back of his mind there was a German Shepherd back there ready to attack him.

He checked his watch and noticed that it had been over half an hour since he had checked in, this would cause the team a little bit of worry, but he had to secure the house and get Meat inside prior to making contact with the rest of the team. He tried the sliding back door and to his surprise it was open. He went in the house and went to work clearing the bottom level. He searched every nook and cranny except for the basement, because when he opened the door the smell of death came wafting up the stairs. He closed the door and propped a chair under the knob as a precaution.

He went up the stairs and went to work securing the upper floor. There were three bedrooms and a bathroom, and it looked as if the prior occupants left in a hurry. There were no signs of blood or a struggle, but the smell from the basement still gave him a little bit of concern. Opie unlocked the front door, went outside, collected Meat and got him to a bedroom upstairs. He then went to work making contact with the team.

"Seeker actual, Seeker Recon over… Seeker Actual, Seeker Recon over…"

"Go ahead Recon over…"

"Roger, we have a situation. Meat hit a cable in the road and we had to seek shelter, he is unconscious and I think that his left arm is broken, I will assess after this check, over…"

"Roger, Moon is asking for your location, can you get us a grid over…"

"Roger, grid is as follows…" Opie relayed their grid coordinates to the team, and told Achilles about storing the bikes near the road. He also said if Meat woke up he would try to get the bikes to his location. They were about to end the communication after Achilles told him to hunker down and that the cavalry would be there to collect them in the morning when Opie heard the first howl of a runner. It sounded pretty far off, but that didn't make him feel any better.

"Seeker, we have tangos near our location, we are going to hunker down and try to survive the night. Look forward to seeing you guys in the morning, avoid the city and take the exit with the BP, I cannot remember the number, but it was before the traffic got all jammed up, out."

Opie went to work getting the home secured for the night. He locked all of the windows and doors, drew all of the shades, and placed as many barriers in front of the main points of entry as possible. He then set up a claymore mine at the mid part of the steps in case he needed to blow the stairs or take out a large amount of zombies. He then went to work on Meat.

Meat was beginning to stir, and with the help of a smelling salt that Opie had in his medical kit, he came around rather quickly.

"What happened?" Meat asked groggily.

Opie gave him a rundown of the accident and where they were at, and instructed him to be as quiet as possible because he had heard the howl of a runner. Opie did his best to set Meat's arm, giving him a local in advance to minimize the pain. He then gave him two Motrin because he would need Meat to be able to handle a gun, and if he had a concussion which all of the signs pointed to, he needed to keep him awake.

Opie went into the hallway and found an attic. This might be their only hope if they were discovered, so he pulled the ladder down and cleared that area as well. He then took Meat up the ladder and sat him up with a view outside. The attic had two false windows that faced the street. He gave Meat his .45 and told him to keep his head down. Opie pulled the ladder up and they hunkered down for the evening.

The Rest Area

At the rest area the team was set up for the night. They refueled the Hummers with the last of their fuel cans and knew that they would have to find some gas in the next couple hundred miles. They knew this coming into the mission, that they would have to find enough to fill both vehicles and all of their cans two or three more times during the trip.

They talked about what they were going to do in the morning; they would strike out at first light and head for the other two members of the team. The quicker they got to them, the quicker they could be on their way. This easy recon mission had gone to shit, and Achilles was pissed that some jackass had put a cable up on the road. That meant that they might have to deal with some locals that were bandits or even worse, trash that took from others and used the current situation in the world to work in their favor. He knew deep down inside that people were just trying to survive, but once the order of things is disrupted, the world falls apart.

They secured the door to the men's room and lit it up via chemical light, then they all settled in to try and get some sleep. They knew in the morning that things could go from bad to worse, and they all wanted to get their teammates out and get back on their way to completing the mission.

Opie and Meat

Opie and Meat heard the howls and then the moaning. Opie looked out the window with his goggles and almost shit himself. There had to be hundreds of them. They were everywhere and they all seemed to smell the flesh of the soldiers, but they were having trouble locating it. The dead started to break the windows of the houses around Opie and Meat, including the one that they were holed up in. Meat was feeling delirious, but Opie still put his sidearm in his hand. Opie was pretty sure that they were safe in the attic unless the dead tore the house down; if they did that, then they would be screwed anyway. He positioned all the gear that

he had between him and Meat and got ready to
fire if the Z's came through the attic opening.
He thought it would be highly unlikely that the
Z's would be able to pull the ladder down and
operate it, but you could never be too careful in
a situation like this.

He spoke in hushed whispers over his
throat mic, which amplified his voice so that
Achilles and the team could hear them. He gave
them a rundown of the situation, the amount of
dead that he could see, the way that they were
tearing the houses around him apart seeking the
soldiers, a rundown of their food and water
supplies, Meat's condition, and amount of
ammunition they had left between them. He
knew that if the house got torn down badly
enough that the attic would not provide them
with sanctuary. He was determined to go down
fighting, all the way to the last bullet he had,
which he would save for himself. That really
sank in. He was Catholic and believed that
there was no place for a suicide inside of God's
Holy Gates, but he would take his chances with
God rather than be eaten alive. He shuddered.

Opie peered out through the window.
There were runners in the street and they
seemed to be looking straight up at the window

he was looking out from. They were grunting and almost seemed to be pointing out direction to the shamblers, and almost as one all of the zombies in the area started streaming into the structure looking for the two-man team. It was unnerving to say the least. Opie thought out all the possible scenarios in his head. He looked left and right and finally found a vent hole in the side of the house. He moved over as quietly as possible and had Meat look out the window to let him know if what he was about to do had any effect on the horde that was outside.

Opie used his multi-tool to pry the vent window back, then pulled out the two Style 4105 Flash Bang Grenades; he pulled the pins and tossed them both outside into the adjacent yard. He hoped that when these went off they might redirect the masses of undead and buy them some time. He would then throw the four M-67 fragmentation grenades that they had between them to try to blow as many of these bastards to hell as possible.

The flash bangs went off and the runners went ballistic. They were literally throwing the shamblers out of their way to get to the source of the sound and light. Meat let him know that it was working, and Opie readied the frags that he was about to toss. He watched as the undead pushed one another aside frantically to get to the light source that had appeared and then vanished. He knew that it was a long shot, but it was the only thing he could think of at the moment. It was still six hours before the sun would rise, and probably eight before the team could get there to help them out.

Opie waited as long as he could; he wanted to take out as many as possible. After this he would have to go to guns, and that would be a no shit scenario. He did have the claymore on the steps, but he was apprehensive to use it. It might destroy too much of the house and they would end up opening a whole new can of worms at that point. It would be a last option, but at least it was there if they needed it.

The Rest Area

The team was getting no rest. They knew that they had two members out there in Indian Country and they had no way to help them. Going after them at night would be suicide and it weighed heavily on Achilles' mind. Sometimes the burden of command takes a heavy toll on those who are in charge. Both of the team members that were out there right now knew the danger, but they were also his responsibility. According to the PAD device information and that of their watches, the team knew it was six hours before they could venture out and be of any help to the guys. They had to be patient and wait, and Achilles also knew that no matter what, the research from North Korea was more important than the guys in the house. This was one of the things that kills most leaders and causes things such as ulcers and stress-induced health problems. He knew it, didn't like it, but accepted it.

Opie and Meat

Opie lobbed the first of the frags outside into the heart of the herd; the blast was loud and shook the house. He could hear the destruction and also the pieces of flesh and body parts hitting the adjacent house. He waited three seconds, looked out then tossed the second one. He achieved much the same results, and the howls and screams of the runners went into overdrive. If all the zombies in the area weren't here by now, they soon would be. The sound of the blast and the wailing of the runners was a lethal combination of ringing the dinner bell to any undead that wasn't already with this herd.

Between Opie and Meat they had 600 or so rounds of 5.56 for their M-4's, and 300 rounds of .45 ACP for the H&K's. He attached the silencer to the handgun and went to work with slow but precise headshots into the zombies that had converged in the backyard of the adjacent house. He did some quick math. He knew that if he fired every five to ten seconds that he would be out of ammo for the handguns in roughly half an hour. He would then have to hunker down and conserve the ammo for the M-4's for a final stand if it came to that. He looked out at what was left of the herd and knew that there were still too many to count. He hoped at least he had gotten most of the runners, as they had been among the first to swarm to that yard.

The zombies outside looked confused as to where to look for the source of the shots and explosions. They had always found the food when this happened before. Where there was loud noise there was food. They were milling about, moaning and searching. It seemed as if the night would never end as Opie watched this all happen.

Opie moved back over to Meat and checked on him. He was doing better but still looked out of it. He was cognizant of what was going on, and Opie fashioned a sling to support his broken left arm. He gave him another painkiller and propped him back up, then gave him some water and checked his vitals. All in all Meat was doing pretty well for someone that had taken a header on a motorcycle just a few hours earlier.

Opie checked outside and the undead were still wandering about. They almost looked confused about what to do next. The runners that were still on their feet looked bewildered. He wondered if they had the mental ability to realize that they had lost some of the others like themselves. He also wondered if the smell of cordite and the burning remains of dead zombies might be masking the scent of the soldiers. This was an interesting development, and Opie hoped that it would help them survive the night. It was 0245 hours, three hours until the sun would actually start to rise in the east.

The Rest Area

The team was finding it hard to sleep. They all had been through situations like this before, but Moon was on red alert. He was mentally running down the route that Opie and

Meat had taken, and was looking over the data on the PAD to get the team there to help their brothers as quickly as possible. He went over it with Achilles and they decided that it was the best route they could take.

Achilles took the chance to contact Opie and get a sitrep on what was going on. "Recon this is Lead over…"

"Go ahead Lead…"

"Roger, how are you guys fairing, over…"

"Lead, we are holding our own, I estimate seventy-five or so have been taken down, took out most of the runners with Flash bangs and frags, over…"

"Good to hear, we will be there as soon as we can, can you give us a lay of the land, over…"

"Roger. As you approach we are in the first brick two-story structure, there is a white vinyl privacy fence in the back yard, break, we are in the attic, break, claymore set up on the stairs for remote detonation if they swarm the house, over…"

"Roger, we will be moving at 0545, expect us by 0600 pending no hang ups… out."

Achilles gathered the team and went over what they knew. Big Joe, Achilles, Woody, and Moon would go in and get the team. Big Brown and Mac would man the sniper rifles and provide over watch for any stragglers and take them out. B and Doc would man the turret weapons to lay down a wall of fire if needs be. They also found a route around the area to get back on the road and moving to their next destination. Achilles knew that they would have to stop to treat Meat, but he would have to hold on until they could get to another secure area.

Opie and Meat

The time was crawling by. Opie kept looking out both of the openings that he could see from. The undead appeared to be ready and willing to wait them out. He hoped that they would just disperse with sunrise, but he knew that there was no way that he could be that lucky. Things had quieted down as far as sound from the runners, but the moaning from the rest was almost enough to drive him crazy. He knew that he was coming down from the adrenaline rush that comes with combat, but also knew that he needed to keep a cool head. Meat was in and out of consciousness; Opie woke him up every quarter hour to keep him from slipping into a coma from the concussion.

Things stayed relatively quiet until 0530, which is when the undead went into overdrive. They started tearing the structure next door apart. Some were searching the house that Meat and Opie were holed up in, but the others were concentrating on tearing the neighboring house into pieces. Opie used the opportunity to lob another frag out into the crowd that was trying to get into that house. It was as effective as possible. The fragmentation grenade only has a 5 meter kill radius, but it still was devastating to the ones that were caught up in the middle. The remaining runners howled, screamed, and went crazy. It was if they were caught up in the dying of their undead brothers and sisters. As Opie tossed his last frag out, Achilles came over the radio.

"Recon, this is Lead, we are en route to your location. Hang in there, we are coming, over…"

"Roger, we are out of grenades and down to 5.56 at this time…"

"Roger, be there in fifteen mikes, over."

Opie started to go to work with his M-4 taking out targets with lethal precision. The sun started to rise, and almost as one the undead looked to the sky. The runners got even louder. It was as if they were exhorting the shamblers to work more quickly. The slower ones went to work on the structure that Opie and Meat were hiding in. Opie could hear the house being torn apart on the first floor. He hoped the team could get to them soon, because he didn't know if the Z's could really take an entire house down, but they had gotten awfully close with the house next door.

The Team

It took them almost half an hour to navigate their way to just outside the neighborhood where Meat and Opie were holed up. They stopped at the motorcycles and loaded them up as fast as they could. Achilles then had them take the vehicles up to about 400 meters from the structure. They could see the masses of undead and all they could do was stare in awe that Opie and Meat had held out for the night.

Achilles reached out to Opie. "Recon, we are 400 meters to the west of your location, we are moving in and will need you to get things loud to cover us coming in. We will clear the backyard and try to come in through the back door, break, do you know how many are in the house, over…"

"Roger Lead, I will look out of the attic and try to get a lay of the land downstairs. I know they are doing their best to take the house apart and the owners are going to be pissed, over."

This made the team laugh. Even in the face of death Opie was still making a joke to cover up for the fear and apprehension that he was feeling.

Opie and Meat

Opie pushed the ladder a little to crack it open and take a look. What he saw was disheartening. There were at least twenty undead in the hallway alone. They seemed to be everywhere. That was the best view he could get for the shooters that were getting ready to come and get them out of this mess. He knew that getting out of here was becoming less and less likely. He spoke on the radio to Achilles.

"Lead, we are screwed, there are at least twenty upstairs, unsure of the amount in the house, recommend you guys abort and head out on your own…"

"Negative, we will be in there to pull your asses out, this is not up for discussion!"

"Roger Lead, diversion will be out when you call for it, we have one more frag, over…"

"Roger, we will call for it when needed, out."

The Team

Big Brown came up with a sound idea. "Sir, I can lead them away, let me take the bike and draw them out. I can meet you guys later and we can get out. I'll ride up there, try to get them to come after me and keep moving back in this direction. Maybe I can at least get them to where we can mow them down with the Ma-Deuce and the 240."

Achilles thought it over. It was a simple plan, but he didn't want to lose anyone. He had to make the decision and make it fast. He nodded at Big Brown. They got the bike off the back of the Hummer and Big Brown took off at a slow pace. He was being careful not to hit another damn cable, but also needed the team to get into position to get Opie and Meat out.

Extraction Team

Achilles, Moon, Big Joe, and Woody worked their way through the field to the back of the house. They all readied grenades to throw over the back fence to provide enough of a diversion to draw as many of the undead to the street as possible. The fewer that were inside, the quicker they could get Meat and Opie out of the attic. They stacked on the fence and Achilles reached out to the other three elements of the team that were in the area.

"Ok guys, I need a go from all elements to start this party, over…"

"Support ready!"

"Big Brown ready to rock and roll!"

"We are ready in the attic for you to save our sorry asses…"
"Roger, commence in 5!"

The three elements in the neighborhood lobbed their grenades out in front of the house as Big Brown unleashed hell on walkers in front of the house with his M-4, more for a diversion than trying to pick them all off. Two runners screamed and took off in his direction.

"Lead, I am on the move, I have runners coming after me, they are streaming out of the house, I'm out of here! Over…"

"Good Luck, Support, be ready to help him out…"

"Roger."

With that, Opie was getting Meat ready to move. He was at least conscious at this point. He could hold the .45 with his good arm and could fire behind them if needs be.

Achilles and the other three men opened the gate to the backyard and went to work clearing it with extreme prejudice. They had six targets in the backyard, and they were down within seconds. The team could see the undead streaming out the front door, since the sliding back door to the house had been shattered by the walkers that had come to the back looking for the scent of the flesh that they so desired. Achilles and his men entered the house and started taking down walkers. There was a close call right when they went through the door; Big Joe was almost grabbed, but without a moment's hesitation he punched straight through the head of the Z. The rage of battle seemed to take control of all of them. They dispatched ten walkers and a runner in the bottom level. Woody grabbed the claymore that had been knocked over. Good thing that Opie didn't blow it as it was aiming straight at the ceiling and most likely would have killed them both. Moon and Woody took up positions at the front of the house and set up the claymore to cover their retreat to the vehicles.

Big Brown

Big Brown gunned the engine and rounded the corner. He had a 75-meter lead on the two runners; he turned back and fired a few shots at them in an attempt to hobble them. They kept coming and with one shot he hit the lead runner in the leg, severing it just below what was once a kneecap. He gunned the engine and took off for the support vehicles and the safety of the larger vehicles. He heard the reports from the Barrett and the M-24 almost simultaneously. The next thing that he heard was Mac telling him his back was clear. He rode back to the vehicles in order to get into the other turret adjacent from Dr. Baker. He was a little disappointed because he had to get in the one with the 240, not the .50 cal.

The Extraction Team, Meat and Opie

Big Joe and Achilles went up the stairs. There were still six of the undead gathered under the opening to the attic, so they both aimed. That was when the floor creaked. The walkers turned their heads as one, Achilles and Bog Joe opened up with their silenced .45's. A few more staggered out of the rooms with their slow gait, and they were taken care of. Opie opened the attic and Achilles pulled the steps down. Opie looked like hammered shit, but he had a huge grin on his face. They helped him and the gear down while Big Joe went up to collect Meat. He emerged a few seconds later and they helped him get Meat down so that Big Joe could carry him back to the transport.

Woody yelled, "We need to move, they are heading back. Let me know when we can withdraw and I will blow this claymore!"

They hastened down the stairs and found that Moon had moved to the back and was scanning the area. They all got ready to exfil and Achilles let the support team know to get ready for them to be inbound. As they exited the back of the house, the first runners were coming from the street to the inside of the building. It seemed to Achilles that they were deliberately trying to stay behind the slower ones to try to stay out of the sights of the shooters.

They exited the fence and Achilles told Woody to "blow it!" Woody hit the remote. There was a load and air sucked out from the lungs of the team; the concussion from the little bit of back blast that came through the house caused them to stumble a bit.

If they were still there to see it, they would have known that the claymore took out hundreds of the undead that were making their way back to the house. There were a few secondary blasts that went off to add to the confusion, as propane tanks that were next to some of the houses or still connected to grills went off one after the other. The zombies were all but decimated.

The team got back to the vehicles, and gently placed Meat in the back of Vehicle Two. Big Joe and Opie got in which left Woody and the Doc to trade places and get into Vehicle One. They turned south by southeast and went on with skirting around the remainder of Boise, Idaho. Achilles knew they had been lucky and wouldn't let the team become complacent in this new and dangerous world again, not while they were under his watch at least.

Chapter 23

Survivors

They made their way to outside of Ogden, Utah. It had once been a stopping point for Mormon travelers on their journey westward one hundred or so years ago. They made their way to Fort Buenaventura State Park. It had been a fort constructed as the white man was spreading the expansion of the nation. They came to a visitor's center which fit their qualifications for a safe house for the night, and went to work on clearing it. They used their standard clearing techniques and found the place to be empty. The only thing that was out of place was that it looked and smelled as if someone had holed up in the building and cooked food in here; they could all smell the aroma that was left over from the previous inhabitants.

They positioned the vehicles facing out the front doors and took their gear inside. Meat and Opie were wiped out, along with most of the rest of the team. Achilles told them to get some shut-eye, and he and Moon went to work on establishing contact with Cheyenne. They gave Honcho a rundown of the situation and explained that they should be two to three days out, five at the most barring any more of the undead that they might encounter.

Big Brown woke up with a shiver down his spine. He could see that Moon had gone to sleep and that Achilles was working on the radio. He went over and asked what was up. Achilles told him that he was calling out on random frequencies that he knew would be used by anyone with a working radio, in an attempt to contact other survivors. He also elaborated on how it was odd that so far they hadn't come across any groups of people just out of circumstance. They sat there for a little while and finally decided that they should eat something. They joked about the MRE's and how they would probably survive longer than the zombies.

A short while later, Achilles was looking out under the vehicles and saw movement. He put his food down and was moving across the room in a flash. Big Brown was immediately by his side with his weapon in hand. They weren't sure if it was a survivor or a zombie, so they took it slow and easy.

Achilles cracked the door and kept it simple. "Hello out there," he said in a hushed tone. He could hear the scurrying of human footsteps and he and Big Brown went outside, using extreme caution.

They emerged from the structure and saw that the daylight was starting to fade to dusk. As they rounded the corner, they were told not to move another step. A man in camouflage hunting gear with a 30/30-lever action rifle was aiming right at them. Achilles lowered his weapon and told the man to take it easy, they were here to help, and they wanted no trouble. He didn't mention the fact that the rest of the team was inside, and probably sleeping still. The man told them to holster those pieces and asked who they were.

"Well sir, I am Colonel Achilles of the United States Army. We are heading back to Cheyenne Mountain to deliver some research to hopefully help out with this problem that we are facing."

It was simple and to the point, he didn't elaborate and kept an even tone the entire time. The gentleman looked them over and let out a whistle.

"Well sir, that sure is some heavy duty hardware that you have on those there trucks. We sure could use those weapons, and I think that we may need to discuss you leaving them with me and getting back on your way." He looked at them menacingly as he finished this speech.

Achilles shook his head. "Sir, we cannot do that. I am sure that we have some gear we can give to you, and also try to get some help out this way. To be honest I have been through more in the last few weeks than I care to discuss, but I will tell you one thing, those weapons are staying on those trucks and going with us."

The man looked down and spit on the ground. He had no clue that Big Joe was coming up behind him. Big Joe grabbed the man and disarmed him, which is when things almost got hairy. Two more gunmen came running out of the woods with their weapons up, yelling to drop their dad. The young men couldn't have been much more than 15 years old, both armed with shotguns. Achilles raised his hands and told everyone to calm down. They could settle this with no gunfire and everyone would leave here with their heads still attached to their shoulders. The teenagers each took a deep, shaky breath and rethought the situation, then at a nod from their dad they lowered their weapons.

Since nightfall was approaching fast, Achilles suggested that they all go back into the building and talk the situation over. They went inside and the father and sons got a full rundown of what was going on.

Achilles spoke to them about the wall that was being built, and how the government was searching for survivors to move up to

Canada. He didn't tell them much about their mission except for the fact that they had research that they were trying to move to Cheyenne. He told them that the President was still alive and that there would hopefully be a new nation comprised of survivors from both countries.

The man's name was Bob. He and his two sons Bobby and Austin had been taking shelter here the night before. Their story was the same as many others, they had left home in search of food and security. They were with a group of survivors that had taken up residence inside a gated community that had over two hundred survivors. They had been out hunting for food when it got too close to dark and they had to take up shelter here. Bob told them that they were only a mile or so away from their community, and that the team would be safe there.

Achilles questioned the man about why he had tried to get the drop on them. There was no reason to try to take on men from the government. Bob told them about the things that had happened over the past year or so. The story was long and the team listened intently to what Bob was telling them.

They had been living in Arlington Woods for the past two years. The community had come together and Bob had heard about it on the short wave radio. The local Sheriff lived there and made it safe. They had constructed towers and had an 8-foot high brick fence completely surrounding the neighborhood. Everyone was doing their part, people were farming crops, hunting, and scavenging the surrounding area to feed and supply the community. They even had an election and the Sheriff was named the mayor. They had a security force, everyone had a place to sleep and they even had generators so that they could take baths. They had some encounters with smaller herds of the undead, but those were never able to get past the wall. The Mayor decided that they needed to increase the security of the area so they built a moat and even another fence as a precaution.

Then one day a convoy of twelve vehicles pulled up and demanded entry. They claimed to be part of the Army, but the Mayor didn't fall for it. All of their uniforms were wrong, Hell, even a dummy knew that much. Their leader called himself General Jackson.

Bob paused for a moment to gather his thoughts, then continued. "He was a large man, and even while our lookouts had guns on him, well, he showed no fear. They came around three months ago, and ever since then they have killed or harassed our hunting and scavenging parties. We knew he wasn't a general, Hell, he was only about 25 years old. To make it more obvious, he carried a big Colt .45 Python on his hip like a gunslinger. Everyone knew his ruse; we had seen people before claiming to be government types, but this man won't stop until he has what is ours. He has a stronghold a few miles up the expressway. His men have taken over a large hardware store and they control the road. I'm surprised that you didn't come across them on your way in here."

Achilles weighed it over. They had a moral obligation to help these people. They needed to get the research back to Cheyenne, but they also couldn't let this happen. They had all taken oaths to support and defend the Constitution of the United States, against all enemies, foreign and domestic. They settled in for the night and Achilles spoke it over with the team. They all felt the same way; they needed to handle the situation if these people wanted their help. They only had around 400 miles to go, but were in need of supplies and fuel. He had Moon get on the radio to put him in touch with Cheyenne.

"Cheyenne, this is Seeker Actual, over…"

"Go ahead, Honcho is on the line…"

"Roger, we are at Ogden, 400 miles to go. We have encountered a large community of survivors, break. They have a local issue with people posing as military, break. We need fuel and supplies, break, we plan on helping them out, break, how copy?..."

"Good copy, we trust your judgment and recommend that you do what you can, but do not compromise the mission, break. Good luck, see you in a few days, out."

They slept well that night; there were no issues with the undead. They thought they heard the wailing of a runner or two, but they seemed to be well off in the distance. During the night Moon was able to get a feed on the radio. He woke Achilles and they listened to what was being said.

"General, we know that they are getting weak, our source inside says that they have most of their hunting parties out right now, so they may be weaker than usual. It might be a good time to hit them and hit them hard!"

The General responded excitedly and ordered all of the men to head back. They would get ready and hit the community tomorrow night, and this time the little fortress would be his!

Achilles asked Moon if he was recording, and he acknowledged that he was. They would use this information to speak to the Mayor and try to get a little bit of good will out of him. They would offer their services and try to help these people out. Anyway, whether it went good or bad, the team would give them the information and maybe they would have time to get ready for an attack.

In the morning they were up and ready to move. Bob rode in the front vehicle while his kids made their way back to the Acres, as he called it, on foot. They had a cache of food that they needed to bring back, and the man didn't want it to go to waste. As the team navigated their way to the community they could see a flurry of action as soon as they spotted a tower.

They approached the front gate to see at least ten men armed with shotguns standing inside the fence. They would need to cool this situation quickly. Achilles told the team to be ready, but to keep their hands off of their weapons. Bob got out of the vehicle and went to the gate. He spoke to the Mayor for a few hushed moments and then he walked back and asked for Achilles to come with him. Achilles grabbed his M-4 and opened his microphone so that the team could hear everything that was being said.

The Mayor came up and shook his hand.

"Hello there, Colonel. Bob tells me that you guys had the drop on him and let him live. He also told me that you have some information vital to our security and that you have been in contact with the President?" This last bit was said in some disbelief.

Achilles shook his hand, introduced himself was and continued to be vague about their mission. He told the Mayor everything that he had told Bob and his boys the night before and then offered the team's help. The

Mayor thanked him for his honesty and invited him and his team inside.

They went in and the survivors of the community closed the gate. The next two hours went by quickly as a flurry of information was exchanged and they worked and reworked the plans that they were making.

Achilles told the Mayor what a good thing he had done for these people, and pumped him for more information about the General and his men. He got a number on their size, vehicles and weaponry. He then asked the Mayor how he wanted to handle it. The Mayor looked like the last three months had taken a heavy toll on his psyche. Achilles could see the stress that these people had been through by just looking and listening to the Mayor. Part of the job of Special Operations soldiers and in particular that of the Green Berets was helping indigent forces to organize and provide resistance. This had been their mission since the government created these specialized units.

Achilles played back the audio that Moon had recorded and they made a plan for the attack that they had heard about the night before. The Mayor was astonished and dismayed. He knew that the General and his men would be coming for them, but the fact that they had someone in the community relaying information to the enemy was a serious punch in the gut to the Mayor. He had no clue that someone would be so stupid, but Achilles came up with a plan to rout the saboteur. He talked it over with the Mayor and they set their plan into motion.

They caught a break when most of the hunting and scavenging crews came back into the community before it got close to dark. Achilles put Moon to work listening for radio transmissions being sent out from the Acres, and trying to pinpoint where they were coming from. It was going to be hard since the fake soldiers were not that far away, therefore a small radio could do the job of relaying the sensitive information outside the walls of the community.

They positioned both of the vehicles near the front gate to provide a serious wall of gunfire if the General's men tried to breach the gate. Mac and B would be manning these weapons. Achilles then had his men take up positions on the roofs where they could fire at targets without the need of being in a tower.

They looked at towers as magnets for enemy fire, so they would fire from nondescript positions. They also had the advantage of night vision and laser designators to hit their targets. Achilles wasn't sure how this would go down. Would the enemy troops (for that was what they were) just storm the gates with the vehicles, or try to use sappers to blow the wall? Only time would tell as the fog of darkness fell upon the community.

Chapter 24

The Battle for Arlington Woods

Moon heard the first transmission go out to the General around dusk. It sounded like the man sending it was scared shitless, but it was loud enough for Moon to get a good recording of his voice. Moon laughed to himself, because the man never mentioned Achilles and the soldiers to the General. Either he was stupid or he had been hiding out all day long and hasn't seen their arrival.

Moon took the recording to the Mayor. He was pissed; Achilles could see the rage in his eyes. He asked the Mayor if he knew who the traitor was, and the Mayor said yes, and that he would deal with it. The Mayor gathered up a few men and they took off in three golf carts toward the back of the community. Achilles took the chance to speak to his men over the radio. They all checked in and were hunkered down awaiting contact. He had Woody on the Barrett, and Big Brown had the M-24. They had both proved themselves to be great shots, and Achilles had total faith in them by this point. They had moved Meat into the community center and he was manning a radio from a desk to be combat control for the team. Everything would be relayed though him. He had a map of the community and would send people to different areas to help out along the fence as the need arose.

Less than a half hour later the Mayor and his men came back with a man in handcuffs. His wife was running after them, crying and in hysterics. They brought him into the community center and put the man in a makeshift jail that was no more than a storage closet for supplies. Achilles questioned the Mayor about how he knew who the traitor was so quickly. The Mayor's answer was short and to the point; it was his cousin. They had beat the shit out of him while taking him into custody and the Mayor showed the stress of having to arrest a blood relative that very well may have ruined everything that they had been building here. Achilles could see the angst in the Mayor's eyes, but merely gave him a silent nod of condolence and respect.

Moon rushed in and laid it out plain and simple. "They are coming, Sir. The General just relayed to all elements that they had the green light to take the community and to leave no man alive, to gather the women and to bring them back to base."

Achilles nodded to the Mayor and told him that it was time to go to work. He then went out and took a position on top of the community center, which would give him a good field of fire that covered the gate and the road that led to the community. Then the waiting began. There is always the time just before a soldier goes into battle when they feel the calm before the storm. In recent years, with the amount of ambushes and things such as IED's wreaking havoc on American soldiers, Achilles could feel his own adrenaline pumping and wondered if getting keyed up for action was affecting the entire team as it was him. He felt it when they rescued Meat and Opie but pushed it down and related it to stress that was normal for that sort of action. Most attacks have traditionally come in the time just before dusk and dawn, that is why all soldiers provide security at these times. Old habits die hard for soldiers, and the wait was on.

Near 2100 hours Woody came over the radio. He called out contact at 500 meters and he was picking it up on thermal. The Barrett had a thermal scope attached so that he could pick out targets with quicker precision than if he was looking through a night vision scope. It was great in an urban environment because it helped them to look through walls. He counted forty men coming through the field and moving in a 'ragged formation' as he described it. He told the team that there was no way in his military mind that he considered this group to be highly skilled or trained. He asked Achilles what he wanted him to do.

Achilles told him to wait until they were at 200 meters and to see if they had any support vehicles coming to aid in their attack. At 250 meters out he acknowledged that most of the team had a bead on a respective target. So far the other three sides of the wall were clear. Big Joe and the Doc had reported seeing nothing, and said it appeared clear to them.

"Lead, this is Woody, I have a three man team at 750 meters, I think they have a fucking 60 mm mortar set up. They look as if they are readying rounds to send our way."

Achilles didn't want to take the chance and have these idiots drop rounds on them, so he told the Mayor to hit the lights after he heard the first shot. He told Woody to "take them out!"

Woody fired a .50 caliber steel jacketed match precision round into the head of the man closest to the mortar, and his head seemed vaporize. It would have been better to see under daylight conditions, but it worked out well anyway. The Mayor hit the lights and the perimeter was lit up like an airport. The men in the towers and the team members went to work taking out targets as they presented themselves. The action was over almost as quickly as it started. Ten or so of the General's men made their way to a ditch that paralleled the road and the snipers couldn't get a clear shot at them.

Achilles and Moon went out to check for survivors. There were two whose wounds weren't mortal and they took them back so that they could interrogate them. They brought them both in and the rest of the team maintained security for the next half hour. After that they took turns manning the Barrett and the scope to look for potential enemies. Achilles didn't play games with these guys like he did with the kids from the Shell Station. He was direct and forced the information out of them. One of the Mayor's men had to leave, turning slightly green when Achilles slammed his M-4 down on one of the man's hands to get him to talk.

They spilled their guts. They were no more than teenagers that had been miscreants prior to the end of the world, and had joined up with a man that could get them drugs, women, and food. They told him everything about their base, about the sick shit they would do to men and women, how the General made them find Asian woman so that he could screw and torture them until they were all used up and then fed them to the zombies that they had penned up inside the store. They gave up their numbers, types of weapons, supplies, and anything else that Achilles asked them. When he was done with them, he gave them over to the Mayor and went outside with Moon.

Achilles had Moon get the radio up and told him that he wanted to have a conversation with the so-called General. Achilles grabbed the handset and spoke into it very clearly. "General Jackson, this is Colonel Achilles, United States Army. If you can hear me I advise you to answer…"

"This is General Jackson, and I think that you should so some respect, Colonel, because I outrank you…" The man's pompous voice came clearly over the radio. Moon looked over at Achilles and rolled his eyes.

"OK, General, here is the deal. We are coming for you. I will give you one chance to have all of your men surrender and maybe we will let you live and have a fair trial. With that being said, you will be waiting for us at 0900 hours in the parking lot, with all prisoners and weapons outside. The weapons will be stacked up and the prisoners will be guarding you. If you do not meet these demands we will be forced to do this our way, nothing further, out!"

Moon killed the feed; Achilles didn't want to give this man the time of day to answer what he had told him. He gathered up his men and asked the Mayor to have Bob come and see him at the vehicles. Bob showed up a few moments later and Achilles outlined his plan to the team and to Bob to see if he was willing to help them out. Achilles wanted one of Bob's kids to show them the way to the hardware store so that they could get there prior to dawn. The team would pack heavy and assault the building, taking out the remaining thirty or so soldiers. They would rescue the prisoners and be on their way by the next day. This was the most pissed that the team had seen their leader. Something had set him off and he was not fucking around any longer.

The team, minus the Doc and Meat, would make their way via a creek bed to the town. They would come up outside the store and set up a support by fire position at the front to lure the unsuspecting guards away from the rear assault. Opie would blow one of the service entry doors with a shape charge and they would clear the building. They were going to take the 240 to provide the support fire. Achilles asked if there were any questions. Seeing no hands, he nodded and the team got ready to move. They would need to move out now to make it to the hardware store prior to dawn, and Achilles wanted these bastards to be dealt with and dealt with quickly.

Chapter 25

Counter Attack

Bob had sent his son Bobby to go with the team and show them the back way to the hardware store that the General and his men were holed up in. It made it only a three mile movement. There was a tense moment when Bobby almost fell over a zombie without the use of its legs, but Achilles put it down silently. He was a good kid and probably would be playing some stick and ball sport for the local high school if the world had not ended. It made Achilles wonder if they could ever get things back to the way they were prior to all of this happening. The lives of the children would be changed forever; they were back in what seemed like the 1800's, with a little more advanced technology.

They got to the store at 0500 hours almost on the dot. Achilles had Big Brown move out to a position where he could open up with the 240 to provide a diversion. If he got the chance he would also use the LAW (Light Anti-Tank Weapon) that they had with them to take out a vehicle. The rest of his instructions was to shoot anything that moved and to let the team know if he saw any movement.

Moon, Achilles, Big Joe, Woody, Opie, Mac, and B all got ready for the assault. Opie had a shape charge made to put in the sliding door. They would hit the target fast and hard, the shock and awe of this would provide them with a better opportunity to take people down. This should also warn the prisoners to get their heads down.

Big Brown was in position at 0515. He let the team know that there were six vehicles parked near the front doors. He also gave them the news that there were at least a hundred walkers in a pen where the garden center used to be. He would have to keep an eye on this; if the scum bags let the walkers loose, the situation could go to hell in a hand basket. There were three guards outside that looked to be smoking and trying to stay awake. You would think that these idiots would at least be readying themselves for a counter-attack. He shook his head in disgust.

Achilles and the rest of the team scanned the area for sentries and cameras. They knew that they had electricity inside, as the generators that were running from the far side of the building were a dead giveaway. They took all precaution and moved with deadly accuracy.

They stacked in two teams on the side of the roll up door. Team One consisted of Achilles, Moon, Big Joe, and Mac. Their job was to take out hostiles and cause the chaos. Team Two had Opie, Woody and B. They were to try to find the prisoners and take out any wanderers. Big Brown let them know that he was good to go.

Achilles asked him one final question: Could he get a shot at the generators with the LAW? He got a resounding affirmative. They all goggled up and got ready to blow the door. Big Brown would commence the attack by blowing the generators, then shoot up the vehicles that were in his field of fire. He had eight hundred rounds of 240 7.62 ammunition with him and planned on using every one of them so that he wouldn't have to hump this stuff back to the neighborhood.

Big Brown calmed his breathing and lined up the LAW, hoping for all he was worth that he didn't miss; that would cause the rest of the team to be in deep shit. He squeezed the trigger and the rocket went straight at the target. As soon as it blew he let out the breath that he had been holding for the last thirty seconds. It worked perfectly, in fact it was almost too good as this ragtag band of marauders had all of their fuel in tanks that were near the generators. It blew big time, and he had to cover his eyes. He heard the charge from the back of the store a split second later followed by secondary explosions from what he assumed were propane tanks that the marauders had never gotten around to using. Big Brown opened up with the 240 and started hitting vehicles and walking his fire toward the front entrance of the store.

The assault team went into action as soon as they heard the blast. They were stacked on both sides of the door and Opie hit the remote to blow the shape charge. As soon as he blew it they noticed the secondary blasts that were going off on the far side of the store. Achilles and Woody popped flash bangs and sent them into the store. They went in and fanned out to take down the hostiles that were their objective.

Team One went straight and Team Two went to the right along the outside wall.

Team One

Achilles and his team went straight ahead. They heard gunshots and ricochets but they assumed that they were coming from the front entrance where Big Brown was concentrating his fire. At this point they had yet to find any bad guys, so they continued to move. Under the cover of darkness in the store they made their way towards the front entrance. As they came to the end of an aisle where there used to be cash registers, they saw people cowering behind makeshift bunkers. There was one man standing and yelling out orders. Achilles knew it had to be the so-called General, and he drew a bead on him from 25 meters away.

Team Two

The prisoners were easy to find. They were in the back of the store where the employee break room was located. B knifed a guy that was standing there in the darkness guarding the entrance to the back of the store where the break room was located. There were no other guards, and the three man team extracted the prisoners and let Achilles know that they were mission complete and heading to the rally point.

Big Brown

Big Brown saw that as a result of the explosions, the garden center had been breached, and most of the walkers were on fire and heading toward the front of the store. He let Achilles know that they were inbound and that he was almost out of ammunition. He would fire until he was out, then make his way back to the rally point himself. He kept up his rate of fire and when he heard the resounding click he looked upon his handiwork. There wasn't a vehicle in the parking lot that would ever move again. He didn't get any of them to blow up, but they sure as shit wouldn't be harassing any more locals with these vehicles. He knew he had done a good thing and for the first time since his son had died in Korea, he smiled. He gathered his gear and set about getting to the rally point.

Team One

Achilles halted his men and they all lined up targets. There were fifteen men at the front of the store, but the team had the cover of darkness and the advantage of surprise. Achilles gave a three count with his hand and they opened up. As they started taking targets down the walkers started to come through the doors. At that point the men in the front of the store were torn between shooting in the darkness as an unknown enemy or engaging the walkers. They chose to run and Achilles and his team took off for the back door and the rally point. Mac was leading the way and stopped at the end of the aisle near the door. He aimed his M-4 down the back aisle and started firing. He would stay there and provide security so the rest of the team could get outside and then the last man would cover for him. Some units use the tap the patch method to withdraw, but with such a small element this way would be quicker and more efficient. The team made it out of the building and headed for the rally point.

They gathered everyone up and Achilles counted fourteen survivors. They would need to be checked over and interrogated, but that was up to the Mayor. As far as he was concerned, they had done their part and had taken a bad group of people out. They moved back the way that they had come and by 0800 hours were entering the front gate of the community. Achilles knew that they had been lucky and that he couldn't let his emotions get in the way of completing his primary mission. They needed to help these people, but the research wouldn't take a backseat again.

They handed over the survivors to the Mayor and Achilles asked if there was a place that they could use to get some shuteye. They needed to get rested and prepped to move out in the morning. The Mayor gladly gave them the recreation center and Achilles had the men set up for two hour shifts cleaning their weapons and guarding their gear. They had helped these people, but they had a lot of gear that people would rather have for themselves in these terrible times.

They all got naps in and were feeling better. They had bathed and were getting everything ready to leave in the morning when the Mayor asked if they would all join him for dinner. It was a surprise; the whole community had pitched in. They had roasted a hog, and even had fresh vegetables. The community dwellers and the team had a great evening. They were glad that they helped these people out and were surprised when they found out that most of the survivors had been part of the community in the first place. The night wore on and they all enjoyed life for a few hours. At 2200 hours they called it a night and got ready to rest for the evening. Everything was ready and Achilles established communications with Cheyenne.

"Cheyenne, this is Seeker Actual, over…"

"Go for Honcho, over…"

"Roger, we are RTB in the AM, situation is contained, we are good to go, plan to make it to Cheyenne in the morning…"

"Seeker Actual, we have two CH-47's that will be en route to pick you up at first light. Eagle himself got these birds rerouted to bring you boys home, how copy?"

"Good copy Cheyenne, see you in the morning, out!" Achilles turned and grinned at his team. It was a great ending to a good day.

Chapter 26

Back to The Mountain

At 0830 hours they heard the familiar sounds of CH-47's in the distance. They had set up an inverted Y for the aircraft to land at, and when they were a few miles out Moon got them on the radio. As they got closer the team noticed that they were painted black and had refuel probes on their fronts. This was the first time since they had come into this new future that they had seen Task Force 160th MH-47's. They had extended range and were a little bit newer than some of the other aircraft in the aging fleet of aircraft that the Army had in their inventory.

The two aircraft landed and they proceeded to shut down. The Flight Engineer and Crew Chief came out and saluted Achilles from a distance. After they completed shut down they went to work attaching the slings to the Hummers for sling load transport. It was fortunate that they had brought slings with them, since if they hadn't the team would have had to leave the vehicles. The two pilots came out and shook hands with the team; there was an older pilot and a young guy that looked to be around 20 years old at the most. He was wearing W-1 rank and Achilles asked him what the deal was. Warrant Officer Gillis responded by explaining that he had been a civilian pilot as a teenager and got lucky enough to be recruited to be a pilot. The Crusty CW-4, whose name was Paige Carrabba, was smoking a cigarette. He told Achilles gruffly that it was his job to get these young bucks up and trained to fly these machines.

They spent a little time loading their gear. The crew had brought some supplies for the community for giving the team a place to stay; this also was a gesture to show that the government was still out there, and word of mouth is the best press. They said their farewells and loaded up to get moving. They had a guy who had been in the Army in the 80's who assured them that he could hook up the sling loads. They cross-loaded just in case an aircraft went down. It would be a long flight with the two Hummers hanging beneath the planes, but it was better than driving across the last couple of hundred miles.

A few hours later the Crew Chief informed Achilles that they were close to Cheyenne. Achilles had to get everyone up, since most soldiers go to sleep as soon as they are airborne. He hadn't been able to sleep. The testing and briefings that were to come were on his mind. The mission had been a resounding success, but he had lost one soldier and that still weighed heavily on him. He had a Commander that told him that this stuff happened, and was part of being the leader of men, but it never helped him. Little Brown would be missed.

The two aircraft dropped the sling loads and they landed. They were met by what seemed like half the base. The main doors to the Mountain were open and Eagle and Honcho were standing there waiting for them. The President had a shit-eating grin on his face, and Honcho looked like a proud papa who had just seen his son hit a homerun. The team emerged from the aircraft to the claps and cheers of everyone standing there. The team formed up in front of Honcho and Eagle. Achilles called them to attention, did an about face, saluted Honcho and told him that their Mission was accomplished.

Eagle and Honcho shook all of their hands, and told them that they had of course done a great service to their nation. They led the way inside of the Mountain complex and everyone went back to their duties. They were escorted to an area that was unfamiliar to them; it was not where they had stayed when they had come to on their first trip to the complex. This area was separated from the rest of the facility. Honcho told them that they wanted them away from the general population due to their celebrity status, and of course until they were debriefed and all the tests on the effects of the serum were tested.

Chapter 27

Testing and Briefings

Achilles and the rest of the team spent the next few days in a haze of tests and briefings. He had been debriefed along with the rest of the team for the better part of eight hours the first day that they were back. They went over everything, every single detail was brought back up, the contact with the CIA spooks, the kill of the North Korean Dictator, the sub, the ship, Fort Lewis, Little Brown's death, the herd of zombies outside of the airfield that appeared to be moving north, the rest area, the survivors, the rescue of Meat and Opie, the list went on and on. At first they were separated and they all told their stories. This was standard for all special operations teams at the end of a mission.

The medical testing was where the fun really began. They were asked a battery of questions about what they felt was different about them mentally and physically. The briefing left most of the doctors and scientists with their mouths hanging open in disbelief. These people had been poring over the data that Opie had handed off to a man in a pair of aviator sunglasses when they had first landed at Cheyenne. It was if they were Mercury Astronauts training for a mission in space. The team was put through tests that seemed advanced, and some that seemed archaic. They all felt as if they had become pincushions with the amount of blood that was drawn from their arms. Every drop of urine and every bowel movement were collected for analysis. They knew that this was all important, but it was the last thing they wanted to go through after the amount of time they had spent risking their necks.

The briefing to Honcho and Eagle was pretty awesome. They all attended it and the intelligence folks had put together a magnificent power-point presentation.

"They always love to use power-point slideshows," Opie said as an aside to Moon.

At the end Honcho spoke to the team. "Gentlemen, I know in these dark times that awards are not necessary. It isn't like pinning a needle to your chest will make all of our problems go away; the fact is that these people need hope! We will be awarding you men with citations. I do not want to hear any crap about it being unnecessary, or that it doesn't matter. The fact is you did the nation a great honor, and we will be doing this so that the people that are here at Cheyenne can see the fruit of accomplishments are still rewarded. I ask each of you not to get frustrated with the fanfare. Also, please do not get upset with the testing that still needs to be accomplished."

With that the briefing concluded and they went back to the laboratories to continue with the scientists.

Achilles went through a battery of strength and agility testing. Everything was analyzed, from the amount of weight he could bench press, squat, dead lift, clean and jerk, to shuttle runs, a mile and two mile run times, reflexes, and the amount of time that it took for him to recover. The interesting part was that he never really felt fatigued. His biometrics were measured as well as his caloric intake, and after each test he had all of his vitals checked. During this process he saw the other team members going through the same amount of testing. At the end of the day when they all sat down to eat, they started talking about their day. They had noticed the augmentation in their eyesight, hearing, and sense of smell, and that they seemed not to tire as easily. The oddest fact was that their caloric intake was nowhere near what it was before. They could get by on less than an entire MRE a day. They did require more water, but they knew that during the testing they had all pushed themselves beyond the limitations they had known in the year's prior.

On day seven of their return to Cheyenne, they had to attend another briefing. This one was headed up by the Chief Scientific Officer, who was Doc Baker's boss. Eagle, Honcho, and a few suits were attending this briefing also. The graphs were amazing. The CSO started by taking his glasses off and telling the group that what they had found was astonishing. He went on to explain to the team that they were totally immune to the zombies. They all had a 25% increase in muscle mass, and they could lift more weight than they had been able to before. Of course Big Joe spoke up at this point and said he could always lift this much. The CSO continued to expound on the team's increased abilities. Their senses were on a level that was easily 1.5 times greater than any data that they had on any humans, including Olympic athletes and top notch soldiers. Their stamina and food intake had drastically changed. The CSO looked at the crowd and said, "To be honest, I wouldn't have believed the results unless I had seen it with my own eyes."

The briefing grew a bit somber when he told everyone that they could not replicate the serum that they had taken. For some reason they were missing a key element in the data that the team had brought back with them from North Korea. Dr. Baker raised his hand and posed the burning question that he had been thinking about since they were infected.

"Sir, I think that our exposure to such a high amount of the virus made this work. Did the specimens that we brought back help to prove this?"

The CSO told the group that it had been helpful, but there was not enough tissue to get it to work with what they were trying to accomplish. The good news, however, was that during their research they had pretty much figured out a way to produce a counter-virus that might help to put the zombies down. They were working on bombs that could spread this to the zombie population, the only problem was that it would take a lot of time, and the zombies themselves would have to spread it. The drawback was that unless they were exposed to the counter-virus by sharing a meal (or eating a human at the same time), they wouldn't pass it to one another. It was far different from the common cold or flu bug. Essentially they were working on something that they could use on large groups of the undead. They would continue with the help of Doctor Baker to try to find a vaccine for the rest of the human race.

Eagle got up and thanked the CSO. He then started his own briefing to the team and those who had been let in to the auditorium after the scientific presentation was over. There were roughly fifty or so people gathered to listen to what the President had to say.

"All right, we have estimated that there have been over five hundred thousand people evacuated to the North. The wall is going up and we plan to have most of Canada sealed from the United States by the end of next year. We are training folks to become citizen soldiers. Our ongoing mission will be to recover as many military assets as possible. We will be conducting raids on most military installations as soon as we have the counter-virus ready to drop. Our main concern is getting as many aircraft and vehicles north of the border as possible. We will regroup, and then take back what is ours!"

This got a standing ovation from the room, and then the meeting was adjourned.

On the way out Honcho stopped Achilles and asked for a moment of his time.

"Ryder, I didn't want to talk to you until after you guys came back. I am not sure if you are aware of this or not, but as a young Officer I served under your father. I have watched you grow up and you didn't even know it. Your dad raised you to be a great officer and a better man. He would be proud of you. I want you to know that I spoke to him when all this shit went down. I tried to convince him to get to Hunter Army Airfield and evacuate with the 160th. He said that the Tybee Road was already taken out, and that he would take his chances with his family. I am sorry that I couldn't tell you this before. What I do know is that he said they blew a bridge and had made the island secure. I have no way of knowing if they could have made it this long, but I will tell you that we plan on going to Hunter and Fort Stewart to acquire whatever we can. The President doesn't want us to risk going that far south, he would rather go after the assets in places where snow falls and it freezes so that we won't have to deal with zombies that can move at full speed."

This information was staggering to Achilles. His family could be alive. He knew that it would be selfish to go after them, and probably a death sentence. But he decided that if they went to Hunter, then he would go to Tybee and get his family. If they were dead, it would give him closure, but if they were alive he had to take the chance.

Achilles thanked Honcho and took the information back to the team. They were astonished. He told them about his father's past, about his home, and how Tybee would be secured if they really did blow the bridge. He never got his hopes up, but even the other team members could see that he was a little more excited than they had seen him in the past. Achilles swore to them that if there was any hope, they would go after the rest of their families. He would make it his mission to help his team get closure, to get to their families and either bury, save, or put them down. They all knew that he would keep that promise.

They attended the awards ceremony outside the entrance of the Mountain. The President gave a moving speech that was as much motivational as it was somber. He awarded the Congressional Medal of Honor to each and every team member. They awarded it posthumously to Little Brown. His father accepted the medal with pride.

Achilles was given a chance to address the large crowd that had gathered. He kept it simple and to the point. "Ladies and Gentlemen. Our nation has been attacked by a foe that needs to be stopped. I know that with our dedication we can take it all back from them. I will do my part, my team will do their part, and you will do your part. Together we can do anything! Our mission is to destroy these godless bastards and get back to living!"

The crowd went nuts, cheering and clapping. He had never addressed a crowd this large before. He knew that their mission had given them hope, and he silently swore to himself that he wouldn't let that hope die without losing his own life trying to save it…

www.ingramcontent.com/pod-product-compliance
Lightning Source LLC
Chambersburg PA
CBHW070551130626
46556CB00001B/115